ALSO BY AMY VENEZIA

Grunge & Grace
(The Grace Jackson Trilogy, Book 1)

Cigarettes and Butter
(The Grace Jackson Trilogy, Book 2)

Mercury and Music
(The Grace Jackson Trilogy, Book 3)

MERCURY AND MUSIC

Amy Venezia

Published 2018

by Ra Vision Books

amyvenezia.net

Edited By: C.F. Dick

Cover Art and Format: T. Considine

ISBN: 978-0-692-18754-8

ACKNOWLEDGMENTS

I want to personally thank the following coffee shops for allowing me to sit and write all three books at their establishments- Crema Bakery and Cafe, Stumptown Coffee Roasters, Stark Street Station, Southeast Grind...and to Red Square Café for the brew I would bring home.

This book is dedicated to all the Gods and Goddesses who come to Earth and show us the way back home.

CONTENTS

CHAPTER 1

Grace didn't know where she was. All she could remember was falling asleep and, in what seemed like a moment's time, she found herself sitting in a stark white room. There were round white tables with two white chairs at each of them. There was a white counter and behind it was a white wall with white tile backsplash, all the way to the ceiling. There was a white espresso machine, and on the counter, were two white espresso cups with tiny white saucers.

Grace was sitting at one of the small round tables. The room was completely empty, except for Grace. She felt a moment of panic. "Am I dead??" she thought. Everything was just so...white. And Coffee. Grace did love her coffee. Maybe this was her heaven. Coffee heaven. Before she could get lost in thought, he entered the room.

He was magnificent. He took Grace's breath away. The moment her breath left her at the sight of this beautiful being, Grace knew she wasn't dead. His gait was smooth and effortless. His eyes were cerulean blue as if the Maldives rested in two small pools beneath his eyebrows.

He looked familiar to her like she had seen him in a photo before. It seemed like an eternity had passed before he reached her and yet, it seemed like no time at all. Grace noted the paradox in that.

She felt a knot in her throat as she looked up, staring at him as he gazed down at her. There was a love and a light about him, compassion and a fierceness like Grace had never seen before in all her life as... well... Grace.

He pulled out the chair next to Grace, and when he sat, he made sure he scooted forward close enough for his knee to brush hers. It sent a jolt of what could only be described as Divinity through her.

He smiled a sly smile. Not sly in a mischievous way, but more in a satisfying way.

"I love to do that," he said.

Grace couldn't speak yet; she just blinked.

He smiled and said, "I just love that first moment when two dimensions collide. Even if it is just the brush of a knee."

Grace blinked again. She could feel her cheeks burning a blaze of five-alarm proportions. Not blushing, foolishness.

He looked directly into her eyes like an Olympic coach would into an athlete's eyes before a debut performance. "Hey, don't beat yourself up. Some people actually pass out. You're doing great! Your tongue will return."

He was right. Grace was beginning to feel her ability to think, articulate, and breathe return. She could also tell he was assisting her in some way with this, energetically.

"Where am I?" Grace managed to choke out.

He smiled instantly.

"You know, most people's first question is 'Who are you?'" He looked perplexed for a moment and then added clear as a bell, "You have communicated with others like me before. I get it. You aren't as shocked by me as you are the... whiteness?"

Grace couldn't tell if this was his attempt at humor or not. He looked like he was waiting for her to laugh and again like he was satisfied with his attempt at a joke. She could tell seriousness was his first language.

"Well, um...I would like to know a few things. Where am I? Who are you? Why are we here? And, why is everything white?" Grace replied.

As soon as the sentence was out of her mouth, he snapped his fingers, and the two espresso cups were on the table with steaming espresso.

"What? You expected the coffee to be white too?" he joked, this time quite naturally.

Grace giggled a bit and said, "Yes...I'm quite surprised it has color."

"Well, black is not technically a physical color, nor white..." his voice trailed off like he didn't want to lecture her at all.

Grace smiled, "Okay, since you haven't revealed where we are, but served up a great espresso...maybe tell me who you are?" Her voice went up in tone on the word are...as if she was a bit worried that she was in a way showing a lack of humility by asking him who he was.

He smiled, "Humans...always on a time schedule... always in a hurry..."

Grace smiled back, "And always curious..."

There was a silence between them that wasn't awkward at all, but instead quite beautiful.

She had no idea how much time had passed before he answered with a voice that sounded like thunder booming through the heavens, "I am Mercury, Messenger of the Gods."

Grace froze in time... if time even existed right then.

In awe, Grace whispered, "But you look like... I mean... you look just like... Dean James."

"Grace, you are going to need to prepare yourself for when I tell you why I am here, and what I am about to share with you." His voice became very serious. Not ominous, but serious.

Somehow, his knowing her name and speaking it had taken her to an intense and almost hypnotic place within. She felt dazed. Everything slowed down just a notch, but at the same time, she felt very clear in her thinking.

"Okay..." she said.

“Before I explain things to you, I want to take you somewhere,” he said gently, making sure he looked directly into her eyes. His concise and deliberate words were like small weights keeping her from floating off into another dimension.

Grace felt woozy and began mumbling, “That must be why you are a messenger... you really communicate in a...” Her sentence resembled that of a drunk person.

And with that, Mercury snapped his fingers, and in an instant, everything went black.

CHAPTER 2

Mercury stood next to Grace watching her intently while scanning her to make sure she was holding up. Humans can be compared to space crafts. Sometimes they come apart when they are entering a new realm or get overloaded. Not physically, of course. They aren't going to blow up physically, per se. But it can be dangerous to the physical body. So, Mercury kept a watchful eye on her as she stood next to him, her chin plopped down almost touching her chest. She was so profoundly out of her body at that moment her head could no longer support its own weight. Mercury took one last scan of her being, to make sure all was in alignment, and with that, he snapped his fingers again.

Grace jolted her head up, startled. Her eyes were bulging out as if a shot of electricity had bolted through her. It took her a few moments to gather her senses. Grace was frantically looking left, then right. Up, then down. Trying to focus her eyes. Feel her legs come to. Mercury could feel all of this. Before he snapped his fingers, he had imprinted her being into his field so he could feel and hear her just as she was feeling and hearing herself.

The room was black, and all Grace could see was him standing next to her.

"Where are we?" she asked.

"We are in what humans like to call a parallel dimension. Although, most of you like to say it like it is fiction. It is not. Here we are," he answered matter-of-factly.

Grace looked around, a bit stumped. Before she could look up and ask him why this dimension was all black, Mercury gestured for her to look forward.

Grace turned her head to stare straight ahead, and as she focused on the all-black space in front of her, slowly, she began to see the light and images come into focus.

She stood in awe as a life-sized switchboard appeared before her. It went from floor to ceiling and looked like it was from the 1940's or 1950's. This one was like something she had never seen. It had giant light bulbs, in horizontal rows, from top to bottom. Grace noticed there were only a few light bulbs lit in comparison to how many there were. A switchboard operator was sitting with her back to them. She had dark, shoulder length hair and was wearing an olive-green skirt suit. Grace noticed every detail. She was wearing hose and black pumps. Her hair was shiny and cut in a long bob. Grace saw the woman's long, slender fingers as she plugged into the different holes on the switchboard. As the bulbs would light up, the woman would hunch over as she typed 90 miles a minute. The odd thing about it was that there was no keyboard. Nothing. She was just making a typing motion.

Mercury, hearing Grace's thoughts answered, "She is sending them information. Upgrades, we call them."

"Sending who?" Grace was becoming more confused by the minute.

That's when Mercury turned and looked her deeply in the eyes and said, "The few who are left, Grace." He said it with such a seriousness that it sent chills through her entire being, which Mercury felt. That made him smile. He always enjoyed imprinting a human into his field. He got to feel what humans feel, and that was still amazing to experience.

Before Grace could express her frustration of not understanding what he was trying to show her, Mercury snapped his fingers again, and suddenly they were standing in front of a giant mansion in what felt like the South in America.

The mansion was huge; the biggest Grace had ever seen. It was purple with massive, white columns, with a grand staircase leading up to the house, as if the mouth of the mansion was open wide to all who wanted to venture inside. They stood outside an ornate, wrought iron fence that surrounded the front yard of the mansion. There were giant oak trees with dreamy moss hanging from the branches that looked like curly, grey wigs. In the front yard, Grace could see several newspapers that had been rolled up and thrown into the yard, as if they had been delivered by the paperboy, yet never picked up.

Grace honed-in on one of the headlines. It was as if she had a superhuman vision, seeing that far away and so clearly.

She gasped when she read the headline, "Kyle Kent dead of apparent suicide."

She quickly turned to Mercury and said, "Wait, is this about Kyle?"

Before she could even take her next breath, Mercury gently placed his palm over her third eye area, right between her two physical eyes, and a flood of images started to move through Grace.

Grace began to see the faces of musicians who were deceased. And then she would see flashes of faces that were depictions of the mythological Gods she had studied over the years. Then she saw the faces of little children. Some were tucked into their beds. Some were on their parents' cell phones. She saw a little girl come forward. She took Grace's hand and placed it on her throat. Grace could feel a buzzing that felt like the girl had bees buzzing around in there. Grace smiled as she felt the strong vibration go through her hand, and at that moment the girl looked up at her and said, "There aren't many of us who have the buzzing anymore."

Grace was confused, but before she could ask what the buzzing was, she found herself once again back in the all-white room, sitting with Mercury. She felt like she was in two places simultaneously. It was an overwhelming feeling.

Mercury waited a moment for Grace to settle into her white chair before he spoke.

He spoke slowly and lovingly, "I know this is a lot for you to take in. But we wouldn't be coming to you if you weren't equipped to handle it. You could say that this was your mission before coming into your body as Grace. So, know that what I'm about to convey to you is something you already know, and something you are ready for.

"Grace, the musicians you saw... there's something that most on Earth don't know about them. It has been hidden from the beginning. And it was hidden for many reasons. One, their safety and the protection of their mission. Two, humans were not ready, nor supposed to know. Three, the earth isn't operating at a high enough vibration to even comprehend what I'm about to share with you."

He proceeded slowly, "As you know, and we know you know, music is the most powerful tool of healing and ascension for your third-dimensional planet. It has the power to influence, to heal, to assist, to change, to unite. It holds the ultimate power, over any other force, that the third dimension uses to accomplish these things. More powerful than magic and what you call praying. More powerful than the mind. As the planet has been on its evolutionary track, music has been a guidance and support system. Beginning around the 1900's, in what is called your America, there was a mission. It called for certain beings to come into human form and assist the planet in the next phase of evolution, from that specific location."

He paused to look at her and make sure she understood so far. As he gazed deeply into her eyes, Grace could feel him helping her translate to the deepest part of her existence.

When he felt her catch up, he continued, "There was a Galactic board of light beings... we will use the language you understand and label them as such... anyway, there was much discussion of how best to go about doing this mission to the highest potential possible. In the end, it was decided that some of the Gods would embody the human form and..." again, he waited for Grace to catch up.

Grace, her eyes as big as saucers, understood what was coming next and Mercury flashed a brilliant smile like a proud father upon hearing his child speak her first word.

"Become these musicians?" Grace asked in a whisper.

"Yes. Yes, Grace. Each of these musicians was either a full embodiment of a God or had been touched by one, and therefore, energetically tied with the God for the lifetime," he answered.

"We knew the dangers of the mission. You see, there's a force that is just as much present in the third dimension. We call them 'The Opposing' and The Opposing... well, they're just as much needed for the evolution. They are the resistance to human evolution. The Opening light beings and The Opposing dark beings actually create the catalyst necessary for evolution. One cannot exist without the other. And this planet cannot survive within the third dimension without evolving into higher dimensions. It must continually evolve, or it dies. So, you see, we knew we didn't have long before The Opposing would catch wind of what we were doing. But we also knew it wouldn't matter if they caught wind of our mission. We purposely set things in motion to ensure that what we were creating wouldn't die easily, that is until now." For the first time, Grace detected a hint of sadness in his voice that was undeniable.

They sat in silence. Grace dared not to speak, for fear of losing the concentration she felt so acutely at the moment.

"To make a long story short, The Opposing saw the wave of music spreading around the world and how it was positively influencing people, helping them shake off the confines that religion and idealism had placed on their souls. The Opposing began hatching their plan to destroy our mission. So, you see, some of the beloved musicians your world has cherished over time were taken from their bodies. Some chose to leave their bodies before The Opposing could use their energy and their gift for personal gain. Some stayed as long as they could and fought hard. Others... there are others still on your planet that keep a very low profile of their birthright as a God. They play under the radar of The Opposing and, like the dense beings they are, (Mercury smiled as he said this) they don't pick up on them." Mercury stopped to let Grace digest what he had just shared.

She sat for a bit, gathering her words. Words that Mercury could already hear but let her speak them instead.

"So you are saying that some of the biggest musicians over time were actually Gods in human form? And there is a force that wants to destroy the influence and healing they put into their music? Music that touches the human masses and raises them vibrationally, without them really consciously knowing it?" Grace asked.

Mercury replied, "In an earthly nutshell, yes!" He was relieved she was taking it as well as she was. Although, he was sending her energy to help her do just that.

At that moment, Grace's thoughts went back to the switchboard. "Why did you take me to the switchboard? What was that about?"

"It is the Universal central board of the mission. And the few light bulbs you saw lit are the few children left on the planet that are a part of this mission. They were the last ones to come in. Sent as, what you like to refer to as, a 'Hail Mary'. You see, The Opposing has taken over music in the country of America, as well as some other locations. They are using music to hypnotize, influence and infiltrate. They've taken the energy of the music and are using it for the opposite of our mission's goal," he answered.

Grace looked astounded. "So, you are telling me that those light bulbs, the ones that were lit, represent Gods that are currently living on our planet today, in the form of children?"

"Yes," Mercury answered.

Grace sat back in her chair in complete shock, "So Kyle..."

Before Grace could ask, Mercury answered, "Yep."

"And Cole?"

Mercury laughed, "You're getting it now!"

Grace looked up and pointed at him, "And you looking like Dean James???"

To which Mercury let out a laugh that vibrated throughout the room. "Yes, I specifically came into this world to usher in the energy of the movement you call Rock n' Roll." His smile glistened like the stars in the sky.

Grace was speechless. Then it hit her...

"Did you know I lived in your unit in West Hollywood?" She could barely contain her excitement. She had moved into an Old

Hollywood courtyard of tiny bungalows when she was in her 20's. The one available was where Dean James lived before he died.

"Of course, I did. How do you think you found the place? And that it was available?" His smile became even more magnificent, if that was even possible, his entire being gleaming with pride.

As if what he told her was not enough, this last tidbit of information was about to send Grace into a tailspin.

"Breathe Grace, and look into my eyes," he said.

He grabbed her arms and locked eyes with hers, and with that, Grace instantly felt like he had breathed new life into her.

She could feel herself floating above her body, her physical body that had been lying in her bed this whole time. She could sense Mercury was sending her back. Before he could, she blurted out "Wait! What about the mansion and all the newspapers??"

"In time my Grace, in time," he whispered. It sounded and felt like a lullaby.

Grace could feel herself melting back into her physical body. She tried to hold onto every, last speck of the out-of-body experience she was having until there was not one left.

Grace slowly opened her eyes and, at that moment, she had no idea who she was. Her name. Where she was. What she was.

It took a while for her feeling of being in a complete state of nothingness to quickly be choked out by persona, mind chatter, ego...

Grace ran her fingers through her sweaty hair as she let out a gigantic sigh. She thought to herself, still in shock over what she'd just experienced, “This is why I have never needed to do drugs. Who needs them when you have this?”

Then it hit her...

What in the world was she supposed to do with this?

CHAPTER 3

Grace tried to keep her eyes open; she didn't want to fall asleep yet. She was right in the space of deep meditation and drifting off. For three nights in a row, she had tried to stay in that space as long as she could, hoping Mercury would return. After all, it was in this state he had first come to her. But for three nights now, there was no sign. No matter how much Grace tried to concentrate before going to bed, whether on the white room, the switchboard operator or even the little girl with the buzzing in her throat... there was nothing. Nada. Zero.

Grace really wanted to know what the mansion was about. It was haunting her, literally.

"If I can just hold on for a few more minutes..." she thought as she gave her last attempt at fending off sleep. Her body was stronger than her will though, and she fell into the silent slumber of night.

She didn't know how long she had been sleeping before she became lucid within her sleep. She heard the sounds first before she saw anything.

First, she heard a breeze. It was rustling through leaves. She could hear what sounded like clanking, as if the wind was causing something to slightly open and then shut again. She listened to the strangest music she had ever heard. It was faint, yet she felt it in her heart. And as she tuned into it, she could hear, layer by layer, different beats. Different tempos. Different instruments. Different keys. Different notes. Different styles. Different voices were singing too. And yet, as diverse as it all was, it somehow blended together to make the most magical symphony of sound. It didn't make sense to her. If this were happening in reality, it would sound like a train wreck! But here, in her lucid state, it resembled Divinity.

It was then that the screen of her mind's eye began to fade into a scene that she instantly recognized. Her heart skipped a beat, maybe ten, as she witnessed the tall oaks slowly come to life. The haunting wrought iron fence too. Now she knew what the clanking sound was, as she watched the unlatched gate swing forward with a gust of wind, and then back on the next beat. It too was playing its part of the musical wave she was detecting. So were the wind and the rustling leaves. She could hear each layer so clearly when she focused her attention on a particular element. It was as if there was a giant soundboard in her mind, and she was able to isolate specific parts and then bring them all back together again as a whole.

It was symbiotic. It was mesmerizing. It was hypnotizing.

Grace closed her eyes and was becoming lost in the sound when she heard someone next to her clear his throat.

"Ahem..."

Grace quickly opened her eyes and turned to see Mercury standing next to her. She couldn't remember a time she'd been happier to see someone, and with that, she flung herself toward him, wrapping her arms around his body in an exuberant hug. As soon as she did it, she was embarrassed and quickly let go.

"I am so sorry!" Grace couldn't believe she'd just hugged the Messenger of The Gods like he was her long-lost buddy.

Mercury was smiling; amused. Amused just as much at her embarrassment as he was by her complete abandon of any humility.

It wasn't until after Grace hugged him that she realized he looked different. He had the same stop-you-in-your-tracks looks, but even more intense. His face, more chiseled. His eyes, more bright and piercing. His hair, Fabio-like. He was taller. Broader. He was just like she could imagine the Messenger of Gods would be.

She was still imprinted in his field, so he could hear every observation she was making in her mind.

"You know what really pisses me off?" he asked.

The question took Grace by surprise. Or maybe it was his bluntness.

"Not really?" she replied.

"The way they depict me as this little messenger in stature. I mean, some of those things make me look tiny. They might as well call me 'Mercury, Fairy of the Gods.'" He seemed genuinely agitated at the thought.

Before Grace could respond, Mercury continued talking. "I guess I can't blame them. I've appeared in a variety of forms. For some reason, the little guy is the one they use to represent me."

"Hmm... you know what they say... don't shoot the messenger. Maybe news is better received from cute little messengers rather than giant and intimidating ones?" Grace spoke before really thinking.

Mercury laughed as he put his arm around her shoulder. Grace thought maybe he was finding her descriptions humorous until he replied, "Oh silly Grace... as if they could shoot me."

This made her smile, which again prompted that silence between them that was so beautiful.

They both stared ahead at the massive mansion before them.

Mercury didn't speak, nor did he move. Grace felt he was waiting on her for something. All she could think to ask was "What is this place?"

Her question must have been good enough because Mercury immediately answered, "This... this is the House of Music." He waved his hand in front of him like Vanna White presenting the next phrase on Wheel of Fortune.

Grace couldn't help but laugh that the mansion before her, the one that easily took up several city blocks, was being called a "house."

"What are all the newspapers for?" Grace asked.

Mercury smiled, arms crossed, amused as he said it, "Oh those? Those are the newspapers reporting on their deaths. They think it's funny because none of it is truth. In a way, it is their...what would you say?... middle finger turned-up at the absurdity. They refuse to pick them up, open them, read them or pay them any attention. And so, each one just sits in the yard for... well... forever... to be eternally ignored."

"That is some funny shit." Grace responded and then quickly put her hand over her mouth like 'oops.'

He laughed at the ridiculousness of her 'oops,' "Don't worry, cursing is permitted here."

Grace could feel her heart beating faster at the thought of what it might be, "So if this is the 'House of Music,' what exactly goes on inside of there?"

"You will have to go inside to find out," Mercury replied.

"I thought you were the Messenger? Doesn't the 'Messenger' give information?" Grace acted out exaggerated air quotes on the word messenger.

Mercury stood, arms still crossed, not cracking a smile. The very look in his eyes made Grace want to hide beneath anything she could fit under. Just as she was starting to feel a quivering in her lip, Mercury let out a huge laugh.

"Gotya!" so proud of himself.

"Yes, yes you did..." Grace mumbled nervously, still having difficulty making eye contact like he was an alpha dog you aren't supposed to look at directly.

"I'm messing with you, Grace. This one is not for me to tell you, but for you to discover for yourself. In time. When you are ready." As he said this, he began to fade, a smile on his face and a twinkle in his eye.

Grace was left standing alone.

She didn't know what to do, but she knew what she had to do. And with that, she flung open the gate and walked through. If anyone could see her from the enormous windows, it had to be a humorous sight. It was as if she was tip-toeing through a landmine, trying not to step on any of the newspapers littering the pathway up to the mansion.

She cautiously made her way up the stairs and to the front door. The door was massive. So large a truck could drive through the opening. Somehow, the knocker was right at her perfect height. And it was a tiger. Grace loved tigers. Odd. Why in the world would they have chosen a tiger as the knocker of this gigantic mansion?

She stood staring, hesitant...and well...scared.

"Times a ticking," she thought to herself, and then instantly thought, "Well, most likely not here."

Before she could stall any longer, she took the handle in the tiger's mouth and knocked three times.

Some time passed, and Grace had no idea how much because it wasn't a tangible feeling here. Finally, the tiny window above the knocker slid open quickly.

A pair of blue eyes stared back at her. She could only see the eyes. She knew those eyes. And in that recognition, her own eyes filled with tears.

There was an awkward moment of silence as Grace waited for him to say something, and yet, he continued staring.

Perplexed by his silence, she asked, "Uhh... hi... are you going to let me in?"

"What's the secret word?" He asked dryly and expressionless.

Grace smiled and said, "Lord, I don't know... umm... Music?"

He just stared more.

"Okay... let me think..." She looked down, wracking her brain. The next word to come to her was one he'd said so many times, and one he used to tease her for because she didn't quite say it as loosely as him.

She looked up, embarrassed and shy-like but begrudgingly said...

"Fuck?"

And with that the door flung open and there stood Kyle Kent with a huge smile on his face like "Thatta girl!!" Arms wide open, he beckoned for her to come in and gave her one of the biggest hugs she'd ever received.

She felt overwhelmed with emotion.

"Oh no... don't do that earthly crap. No crying. No crying, Grace!"

She jokingly slapped his stomach, bending over from the wave of emotion coming over her, and said, "Shut up. I know you remember how it feels. This is some intense emotional stuff happening."

"Psshhh... you're saying 'stuff' instead of 'shit' now? What happened to my Grace?"

"Give me five minutes around you and it'll all return." She laughed as she looked up from her hunched over stature.

"As much as I would like that, no can do. You have to go back."

"What? I just got here! Why??" she asked, clearly upset.

"You took too much time getting through the newspapers. Your time is up." He looked dead serious.

Grace had a shocked and sad look on her face, so much so, Kyle couldn't bear to let her continue to think he was serious and said, "I'm kidding you, but you do have to go back. I can't explain right now. But I promise you, when the time is right, I will get you back here. Promise."

Grace looked up at him, eyes filled with sadness as her throat tightened at the thought of leaving.

He placed his hands on both of her shoulders and stared right into her eyes as he said, "I promise you, Grace." Then he pushed her slightly, to which she fell back into her body and woke up.

For a moment she felt empty and sad. Not only because she'd really missed Kyle, but also because she'd felt at home while at the mansion. Now she was back in a dimension that she loved. Yes, she loved being alive... but it was hard to experience the other realm and not feel sadness.

Her feeling was quickly replaced by a thought that made her laugh...

The secret word.

CHAPTER 4

It took a while for Grace to realize where she was. She was coming out of a groggy sleep, feeling like she'd been drugged. It took some time for her eyes to focus, and to even connect with her body. She concentrated on wiggling her toes, then her fingers as she felt the blood rushing into them like a raging river, bringing them life. Feeling.

When she was fully awake and aware, she found herself in a room. It was the trippiest feeling she'd ever experienced. In one moment, the room felt small, but then she would look forward, and it would look like the place had lengthened and widened all at once. Like, if she wanted it to be small and cozy, it would be, and if she needed more room, it would expand.

The room had wood floors. Old wood floors. The kind she'd seen in old cabins in the Southern parts of the states. One, in particular, came to her mind. It was the servants' quarters of an old southern plantation that played a vital role in the Civil War. Yeah, the floors were just like those. Like, no matter how much you cleaned them, there was still dust. And no matter how much you scrubbed them, they were never going to shine. As if they were like a sponge, absorbing centuries of life, love and death.

There was a small, twin-sized bed backed against a wall in the center of the room. It had a thin tan blanket laying at the end and was immaculately made. It reminded Grace of how those men in the military were taught to make their beds. She was staring at the bed, lost in thought when she heard the strumming of a guitar and out of her peripheral vision saw him sitting on the floor in front of her.

She turned her gaze in the direction of where he sat with his back up against the wall, legs out-stretched, ankles crossed. He was wearing a long-sleeved shirt with a t-shirt underneath it. Jeans. Boots.

He was strumming his guitar and humming. Grace felt like saying "Kyle Kent in the flesh!" but she knew he wasn't in the flesh, as much as her eyes deceived her.

The sound alone was heavenly. Grace felt the music slowly move through her, and with each inch, she felt more and more peace.

Grace sat on the floor across from him in meditation pose. She wasn't sure why she sat that way, but it was just what she felt to do. Grace just stared. There was nothing she wanted or needed to say at the moment. As Grace was deep in thought, Kyle looked into her eyes and smiled a sweet, closed-lip smile. He was still strumming his guitar.

Kyle quickly lifted his eyes to the ceiling, gesturing for her to look up. When she did, it was as if the ceiling had retracted and the tallest trees Grace had ever seen hovered above them, like an evergreen canopy. Grace instantly felt like she was in the Northwest. She recognized those trees. Both the feeling and enormity of them. How brilliantly green they could be, and how magical they were.

He studied Grace, still smiling. She could read a mixture of enjoyment in seeing her reactions and wonder, to pride in his room. And with this thought in mind, Grace asked, "Out of all the rooms you could possibly have, why this one? I mean, it's very peaceful, yes... but it's so minimal." She said this from a place of honest curiosity.

Kyle quietly asked, "Have you looked out the windows yet?"

Well, no she hadn't. Kyle stared at her, waiting for her to take a look. Grace got up and walked to the window above his head. The visual treat took her breath away, out of the absolute beauty before her, but also the feeling it gave her. Outside the window was the most turquoise blue water she'd ever seen. It was calm, and you could see straight through it. It was as if the sky and the sea were in a battle for who could be the most brilliant shade of blue! Grace got a little queasy though, as it appeared they were literally in the middle of the ocean. They were surrounded by water, and it was as if the room they were in was sitting right on top of... well... the sea.

"You get used it." he said softly, obviously feeling her uneasiness. He was just a few inches from her legs, and she could feel a buzz coming off him that was nothing less than electric.

She looked down at him, into his eyes and smiled saying, "I don't think I ever realized how much your eyes match the sea until now."

"They are bluer here." He said in a mischievous tone.

"Ohhh... is that how it works?" Grace asked.

"Yes, everything is more here. More...and brighter...and some may argue, better. But that depends on who is arguing." He said.

Grace went back to sitting across from him, but this time right at his feet.

Grace flashed a little smile, "What is this place? I'm trying not to let on to the obvious, but I feel like a kid on the first day of high school here."

"Do you remember what Mercury started explaining to you the first time you came here?" He asked.

"Yes... about the Gods and musicians?" Her voice trailed off, still unable to fully comprehend it.

"Well, this is where we kind of all hang out. We all have rooms here. Sometimes we are alone in them, sometimes we hang together." He replied, looking at her with a look that Grace couldn't entirely read into at the moment. Then it hit her... what he was waiting for...

Grace teased, "Okay, so I know you're anticipating my next question..."

Kyle bantered back, "Good to know you've still got it. I was beginning to worry."

Truthfully, Grace had begun to worry too. It had been so long since she felt the connection with Kyle like she did at the beginning. It was as if he was far, far away, and although Grace could still feel him... at times hear him... it was in no way how it had been. And truthfully, she had grieved a bit over that.

"You know I left because I had to. It couldn't stay the way it was. I was in danger. You were in danger." He answered in a serious tone, eyes blazing into the deepest parts of her soul. She knew what he was saying was the truth. She had felt this too.

"I know. It still felt like losing a friend. It helped me feel great compassion for the people you knew in life that felt the physical loss of you. I didn't know you in body. And I have the gift of still being able to feel you, no matter how far away you are. I wish I could help them to feel the same." Her thoughts trailed off, a bit of sadness and a bit of frustration along with them.

Kyle abruptly strummed his guitar in minor cords to jar her out of her thoughts, which made Grace jump a little.

She smiled as she said, "Nice. Do that again, and I might have a heart attack and join you here."

It was as if Kyle considered for a moment this might be a good thing, and right when Grace was about to hit one of his boots in protest, he let out a laugh.

"Not your time yet, Grace. But you're welcome here when it is."

The thought hit Grace deeply in a place that brought up a bit of fear and anticipation at the same time. The Afterlife. That was for a whole other time...

"Let's get back on track here...being I have no idea when you are going to kick me out like last time! Were you a God too?" She asked, wide-eyed and in true anticipation of the answer.

Before she got it though, she felt herself crash back into her body, and with such force, it made her jump directly out of bed and onto the floor.

"Damn it!" She thought in frustration. Grace was so close to the answer, and she wasn't ready to leave yet. She felt tears of defeat beginning to well up in her eyes like a child who had been awake too long and needed sleep but didn't want to miss a moment.

That is when she heard him laugh. She felt Kyle swirl around her, like a big brother teasing his sister, saying "You really missed me!"

She wanted to punch at the air - in a playful way, of course - but she was also frustrated.

"We have all eternity Grace. Get some sleep."

At first, Grace wanted to defy the thought of sleep and do anything but that. But then it hit her... an exhaustion deep and all-enveloping. She pulled herself up from the hardwood floor and crawled back into bed.

Right when she was about to drift into a deep sleep, she heard his voice one last time...

"For the record, I really missed you too."

CHAPTER 5

Kyle sat on the edge of what Grace had called his "cot" and stared at the wood floors beneath his feet. His hands were tucked underneath his legs, and he smiled as he recalled her non-impressed attitude towards where he chose to spend time in his 'eternity.' Damn, he'd missed her. Grace was someone he would always be able to recall what it felt like being alive with. She was one of the last ones... the last ones to get to feel that part of his essence before he ascended.

He was worried. Worried Grace wasn't ready. Hell, who *would* be for what she was about to experience? He had felt how much her experience with him had altered her life. He felt how once he showed her some of their past lives together, it was like the last bit of security she had been holding onto dissolved in her very hands. Not because the lifetimes had been awful, but because she was shown something that could blow a fuse in any human's mind.

And then he left. He felt terrible for that. It wasn't an easy decision. In fact, the difficulty in it actually surprised him. But he really had no choice. He was in danger. She was in danger. And there were many working hard to scramble their connection and keep them from communicating. He knew he had to trust Raj. Raj had said that he would be more helpful to Grace as an ascended being, rather than one on the run. And he'd been on the run. He had been swept up by Archangels... legions at times... and taken here and there... just to keep a step ahead of The Opposing. The realms that are closer to Earth are more dangerous.

Kyle fought leaving. He didn't want to lose the physical feeling he still had, even though it wasn't the same as being alive. But it had its perks, that's for sure. He didn't want to leave his children. He didn't want to go before he saw the truth come out. He didn't want to leave Grace. He scoffed under his breath at that one. There had been more than one lifetime where that was the case. It was pure irony to him that he felt it again in this one, as Kyle Kent, when he'd never even crossed paths with her in the physical. He had finally begun to heal with his mother. It took leaving for him to see many things about their connection in the big picture. He was enjoying coming to her and her feeling him near. He was enjoying the relationship he could never have while he was in his body. No, he hadn't wanted to leave her either.

No matter his protest, he had to choose. He chose to listen. To ascend and do what he could from the new realm. One of the things that helped him decide was the disclaimer that he could return at times. And he did as often as he could.

It was during those times he could feel Grace was a bit sad. A bit lost. A bit grief-stricken. Even though in her next moment, she understood he had to go. He didn't want to see her go through anything else.

With that, he got up from the bed and quickly walked to his door and opened it. The door opened to a narrow hallway that seemed to go on for... an eternity. He looked to the left and to the right. The hall had wood floors, and a bright red, Persian carpet flowed down the middle of the hallway, leaving the hardwoods exposed on both sides. It reminded him of a giant tongue unfurled.

He veered to the right, and in an instant he was in the front of the mansion, standing in the great room. And great it was. The ceilings went on into the sky and were painted the most vivid scenes of earth you have ever seen. It struck Kyle as funny that you can go to places on planet Earth and they are painting heavenly scenes on their ceilings. Clouds and angels. Gods and Goddesses. Stars and sky. Here, it was the beautiful memories of everyone hanging out there... of their time on Earth. All their times on Earth. And it was forever changing, like a slide show.

Because Kyle's mind was on Grace, the ceiling was a Northwest forest with hidden lakes nestled deep in the middle of them. It was the greenest green one could ever witness... one of his favorite colors in that lifetime.

He didn't have to say anything or call anyone. His mere projection of current energy and thoughts was enough to summon who he wanted to come forward, and with that, the red-tongued hallway spit out Cole Kitchen. Cole still hadn't gotten used to his 'feet' so to speak, and he almost fell upon landing, which made Kyle laugh.

"Shut up man... it is like getting off a ski lift going at lightning speed!" Cole said teasingly.

Kyle thought that was a great analogy. "You just can't take it so literally, Cole. It's not like you have fucking feet. Just imagine landing, and that is all you need to... land!" He smiled as he said it, patting Cole's shoulder with his hand in a brotherly gesture. The two hugged before Cole spoke next.

"I know why you are concerned. I do. But from what I see and what they have shown me, there isn't much choice man. The time has come, and they will use who they can use. Ready or not." The tone in Cole's voice was respectful and insightful.

Kyle knew what he was saying was true. And before he could answer, Star came flying out of the hallway like a surfer on a giant wave. So slick. So cool.

"That's how it is done!" Kyle said as he gave a side glance to Cole, who was looking a bit ashamed that he still hadn't gotten it down yet.

Star was one of the most prolific musicians to be dispatched as part of the mission. He manifested as male on the planet, but here in the 'afterlife,' he manifested as female and male. Today, he was male. He was dressed in head to toe purple and had a purple boa around his neck and a purple top hat that seemed ridiculously tall. Like almost as tall as he was.

"What?" he asked sheepishly. "I knew Raj would be here, and I can't have Raj outshining Star!" his smile was brilliant as he teased.

He went over to Kyle and gave him a big hug. As he walked to Cole, he patted him on the back before hugging him saying, "You'll get it... you just have to remember you have wings instead of feet!"

They were having a bit of small talk when the ceiling began to part in what looked like a swirling circle in the middle of it. The cyclone-looking circle was spinning faster and faster, and all three were staring up at it when a giant parrot broke through the haze. Giant wasn't even the word. It was big enough to have Raj saddled on the back of it as he rode into the room, and the room expanded to accommodate the size of the massive bird! It was bright green, brighter and lighter than the Northwest pines that once made up the mural on the now swirling ceiling.

"I thought I would have him match the decor," Raj said as he jumped off the back of the parrot and sat cross-legged, levitating in the middle of the air. With the snap of his finger, the parrot disappeared as well as the hole, closing up on a dime.

Kyle, Cole, and Star stared speechlessly. It never ceased to stun them. Even though they were Gods in their own right... Raj was just beyond anything.

Today he wore huge, gold hoop earrings. When Kyle looked closely, swearing he could see something moving on them, he saw tiny monkeys perched on them. Running up, down and around them.

Raj, reading his mind, laughed a belly laugh and teased, "I thought it appropriate to bring monkeys to come see YOU monkeys!"

"Very funny," Kyle said with a smile.

"Now, what can I do to ease your concerns here?" Raj got straight to the point.

They all three looked at each other and felt a little embarrassed for even summoning Raj forward to question whether or not this was a good idea... to bring Grace here to witness it all. In fact, now it seemed foolish... as they all knew it wouldn't be done if not necessary and part of the mission.

Still, Kyle spoke up first.

"I am just concerned for her Raj. I know it is all a dream. I know nothing can ever truly harm us. But this is unprecedented work here... at least in thousands of years..." Kyle's voice trailed off.

Cole stepped in with, "She has already done so much. Gone so far beyond what any of us thought she could."

Star stayed silent as Cole and Kent stared at him like "annnnd..."

If they could have elbowed him, they would have.

But Star still sat silent. Even Raj was waiting for his thoughts.

"I think baby girl will do just fine. I think she's gonna really shine. I think we've gotta trust the time." He began to dance to a piece of music only he could hear.

"And we lost him!" Kyle said laughing.

Star was still grooving around the room as they all were contemplating what had been said.

Raj smiled at him, loving every bit of his groovy display before he said, "We would not do anything that could compromise the mission. In the end, that is all it comes down to. See how easy it is for even you to lose sight for a moment of the truth? Your incarnations are still fresh in your memories. You know it is but a blink of an eye. You know that worry is a trivial way to use energy. It doesn't exist... all that is worried about. You know everything said and done all dissolves in the end, back into the great unknown... or super-unknown as some have called it." He had a twinkle in his eye as he looked at Kyle.

Kyle knew what he was saying was the truth.

They all sat silently, each one staring at different places in the room. Kyle, on the floor. Cole, the ceiling. Raj, straight ahead at them. Star... well Star had his eyes closed, immersed in his own world.

In an almost fatherly tone, Raj suggested, "Look, if you want to feel you are doing something to ensure it goes well, send her extra energy to help her with her clarity." Their loving concern touched Raj. Each one had a different way. Kyle was protective. Cole was hopeful. Star refused to imagine anything but joy and how Grace is brilliantly fulfilling her destiny.

"In the end, it is her destiny," Kyle whispered, now being the one reading Raj's thoughts.

"In the end, it is all of our destinies." Raj matter-of-factly replied.

With that, Kyle looked up, feeling more aligned with that. Knowing he had lost sight for a moment. He had to smile to himself because, briefly, he'd found himself a bit humanlike in thought.

Reading Kyle's thoughts, Star chimed in, out of nowhere, "That Earth... it can really bring it out in us, huh?"

"That Grace brings it out in some of us more than others." Raj teased as they all looked at Kyle as he stated the obvious.

Kyle threw his hands up in surrender, laughing as he said, "Hey, I'm not going to deny it. It's not like I could even if I wanted to."

They all laughed, each of their thoughts drifting off to the earthly beings who did the same for them.

Before any of them could speak Raj snapped his fingers and was back on his parrot in the blink of an eye. He grabbed a tuft of the bird's feathers, and as he was turning it around preparing for take-off through the ceiling, he shouted over his shoulder, "Toodle-oo!"

The three of them watched as the bird got sucked into the cyclone that suddenly reappeared. As if in a trance, they observed three green feathers float down from the ceiling and land at each of their feet.

Kyle bent over, picked up his feather and smiled, "I'm going to get some new inkwells and write with this."

Cole picked up his feather and thought, "I'm going to paint this into a scene."

Star swept his up and stuck it directly into his top hat.

Smiles crossed their faces as they quietly looked at one another with resolve and more peace.

They opened the door to the large hallway and Kyle gestured for Cole to go first.

Hesitantly Cole stepped into the hallway and tripped on the rug as he did.

"Really man?" Kyle laughed as Star just rolled his eyes.

Cole looked back at them with a sly smile and said, "Gotcha!"

CHAPTER 6

Grace awoke on what felt like a cloud and the sounds of someone strumming an acoustic guitar. It took her a while for her eyes to adjust as she turned on her side to see where the music was coming from. Kyle sat in his regular spot, on the floor with his back up against the wall. Legs outstretched, he was dressed in a cream-colored long-sleeved linen shirt, brown cargo pants, and brown lace-up boots.

They just stared at each other. Not saying a word, even though Grace had about a thousand questions running through her head.

He finally broke the silence and asked, "Comfy, isn't it?"

As always, he'd been reading her mind. She was just thinking how shocking it was to be sleeping on a cot with a mattress that was like a Wheat Thin and yet, felt like she was on the puffiest cloud-like bedding in existence.

She smiled as she groggily said, "Too bad they don't sell anything like this on Earth."

Kyle grinned, "They haven't even come close, and probably a good thing. Who would ever want to leave it?"

"And you have a hard enough time getting going in the morning..." he teased.

It was true. Grace was definitely a person who needed her coffee in the morning to create cohesive thoughts, let alone words.

And with that, there was a steaming cup of coffee on a small table next to the bed. The cup reminded Grace of the tin cups she drank out of when camping.

As soon as the thought passed through her head, the roof of the room retracted, and those majestic pine trees reappeared. As Grace was looking up at them in awe, she heard the sound of a crackling fire. She looked forward to see a campfire built right in front of Kyle, in the middle of the room.

"Wow... are we glamping?" Grace asked. They were in a mansion, after all, despite Kyle's minimalist room.

"Technically, we are mamping," he replied.

Grace stared at him, blankly, as she sat up in the bed with her back against the wall.

"Oh come on... mamping... mansion and camping..." he said acting a bit disappointed in her inability to get it.

"Ohhhhh... yes... mamping! Clever... too early for my mind to compute..." she made her excuse for her slow understanding as she took a sip of the best coffee she'd ever tasted.

Kyle smiled, "Good shit, huh?"

“Yes, super good shit!” Grace laughed, trying not to spill it in the process.

“What are you trying to do to me? Cloud-like mattress... Universe’s best coffee... you playing your guitar...” her voice trailed off as she spoke. She was a bit sad at that last part. Not for herself, but for the rest of the world that still longed to hear him play.

As if reflecting on his own feelings he said, “You will still want to go back...once you are gone... there will always be a part of you that will want to.”

They sat in silence. Neither uncomfortable. Neither needing anything other than being silent at that moment... and the next.

Grace watched as Kyle propped his guitar against the wall and scooted closer to the fire, stoking it with a large stick. She had no idea where he’d gotten the giant stick from, but nevertheless, it was in his hand and poking at logs in the fire.

Grace stared at his guitar, almost hypnotized.

“That should've been their first clue, you know,” he said, still staring into the fire.

“What? Your guitar?” she asked.

“The fact that my guitar was laying down. I would never lay my guitar down like that. Not only because I consciously wouldn’t, but also out of so many years of habit,” he answered.

Kyle was referring to the scene of his death, a thought that made Grace sad to even think about.

"We're not here to talk about that." His tone was neutral, not emotional in the slightest.

"Okay... what are we here to talk about then?" She asked, intently staring into his eyes.

"Anything you want to talk about," he said, again in a neutral tone.

For a moment, Grace felt a bit of agitation that her reason for being here was placed back into her court. This was her 3rd or 4th visit back to the mansion, and she knew no more than when Dean James had first started explaining things to her. But that quickly passed as she began to realize all the different questions she had for him.

"Alright then... are you a God?" She came right out and asked.

"Well, don't you get right to it?" he said laughing as if he was a bit surprised by her question.

Grace laughed, fully aware that he was always reading her thoughts, "You didn't see that coming?"

Staring intensely into her eyes he said, "Sometimes I 'unplug' from you; I like to be surprised." It was as if he was communicating a message beyond the words. A deeper understanding.

"Yeah, I remember your ability to unplug Drops of Jupiter. That is pretty amazing you can do that...but are you going to answer my question?" She was smiling as she asked.

"I have been many things." his short reply to her.

"And is a God one of them?" she asked, not letting him off the hook.

"In a way, yes." he answered, flatly.

"Do you remember the past life I showed you in Egypt?" he softly asked her. "The one where you were there too?"

"Yes, I remember... but what you were showing me all happened so quickly. I barely remember the scene... more the feeling." she said.

"That was a lifetime connected to Ra. Do you remember Ra?" He said his words slowly and deliberately. Grace felt each one moving deeper and deeper through her.

"Yes..." was all she could manage, whispering.

He smiled the most gentle smile as he said again, "I have been many things."

They once again sat staring at each other.

"Did you know this when you were in body as... Kyle?" she asked, confused.

"Not consciously, no. But if you look at how many times I talk about the sun in my lyrics..." he said, amused at himself.

"What is the point to all of this?" She decided to just get straight to it.

"This?" he asked.

"If you are a God or connected to one... or whatever... why did you come into the world as Kyle? And all the other lifetimes you showed me?" She was frustrated because she felt like it was way more than she could comprehend.

"For the mission. You do remember some of what Dean told you, right?" he patiently asked her.

"I do... it is just so..."

"Confusing?" he interrupted her before she could finish.

"Look, Grace, this is going to be a lot for you to comprehend. I'm not going to sugarcoat it or blow smoke up your ass. It may feel like your brain is short-circuiting... or you're losing your grip on reality, but you're ready for this. You are. And I'm going to help you through it." He said everything with an authority that made Grace feel comforted and at the same time, safe.

Grace laughed at the irony of the smoke reference, considering they were sitting in a room, watching smoke waft up through the retractable ceiling.

"That's a roof Grace, not an ass."

They both laughed, needing to lighten the mood a bit.

Before Grace could gather her next thoughts, Kyle stood up, and when he did, the fire disappeared. He walked over to the side of the cot and extended his hand. Grace looked at his hand and up into his eyes, and asked, "Where are we going?"

"Do you trust me?" he asked.

"You know I do," she replied.

He took her hand as she got out of the bed and stood in front of him. "Then come with me," he said.

Suddenly, Grace found herself standing with him in a hallway that went on as far as her eyes could see, both to the left and to the right.

Kyle waited for her to get her footing, then all of a sudden she felt them floating down the hallway. It was as if the red-carpeted floor beneath them was a conveyor belt, moving faster and faster. Grace could hear the sound of dance music, similar to something you would belly dance to, and it was putting her into a trance with each and every beat.

The harder she tried to stay in control the more dizzying it felt, so she decided to trust him and let go. She closed her eyes and with Kyle still holding her hand, they moved down the endless hallway. Grace allowed herself to sink further and further into a feeling that could only be described as otherworldly.

It wasn't until she felt the movement stop that she opened her eyes. They were standing in front of an ornate door. It was massive. The wood carvings were the most exquisite she had ever seen. Of all things, there was a unicorn head as the knocker on the door, and before Grace could question where they were, Kyle gave it three loud knocks.

Grace was staring straight at the door when she felt Kyle whisper "Breathe, Grace" into her ear. It was then that she realized she was holding her breath entirely.

She took a deep breath in, and as she did the door flew open and there stood the musician that Grace knew as Star, standing in front of her.

"Well, it's about damn time! Get in here baby girl and let me get a look at that light." Star grabbed her arm and yanked her through the door.

Stunned, Grace turned to look back at Kyle who was still standing in the hallway.

She was perplexed by his look of amusement, and he was amused by her look of perplexity.

CHAPTER 7

Grace had to blink her eyes in rapid succession to even feel like she was still in her body. Just the sounds of guitars riffing in the most soulful melodies and in her line of sight were... well... more than she could take in.

Star stood next to her, his arms crossed and one hand up to his mouth in the most curious pose. As if he was studying her... scanning her from head to toe. He had a sly smile, and his neck was moving back and forth to the groove of the music.

With each second that passed, Grace felt more and more able to focus and come back to her senses. It was then she realized Star wasn't scanning her, he was sending her energy from head to toe.

He smiled as she realized this and outstretched both of his arms as he brought her in for a hug. He was small, but man was he a good hugger. It was as if fireworks went off in Grace's heart. Pure joy was moving through her veins.

"Look atchu. Standing here in my room," he said as he held her back far enough to look her in the eyes. A look of pride on his face, as if she had just done something remarkable and he was the father who got to witness it.

Tears welled up in Grace's eyes. Just from the pure love and joy. From the incredible experience she'd been having so far, and the humility she felt from even being there... much less, communicating with Star and Kyle.

"Oh no, not here baby!" Star exclaimed, and when he did, he whipped out a tiny vacuum hose attached to absolutely nothing and sucked the tears right from her eyes!

This made Grace giggle, which made him start giggling too, and before she knew it, they were both bent over laughing as if they were... well... high. She was high. High on love. On wholeness. On joy. On gratitude. It was the best feeling she'd ever felt.

"Good shit, huh?" he asked her, with a sly smile.

"Funny... Kyle asked me that very thing this morning regarding the coffee," she said. He gave her a look as if to say "duh," and this made her once again feel late to the joke.

"It takes a bit to catch up here... you are doing just fine," Star said as he walked past her.

This made Grace turn around, and when she did, she almost jumped out of her skin! For when she did her face plowed into a ton of feathers. She was spitting them out of her mouth when she realized she'd run into an ostrich!

She backed up to take it all in. The ostrich was pink! Like a flamingo. Its feathers were the colors of the rainbow. It was magnificent.

Grace looked around her to see many of the same ostriches roaming about. They all had tiaras on their heads.

“Crowns, baby girl. Crowns,” Star said, reading her thoughts.

“Can I ask you something?” Grace said.

“Well, that’s why you're here...of course!” he said. Grace could feel he was eagerly anticipating her question, even though she knew he was fully capable of reading her mind.

“Why ostriches?” She smiled an innocent smile as she asked, afraid that maybe there was an obvious reason that she, once again, was not getting.

“I get them, baby. All my life I wanted to fly. I remembered flying. I knew what it was like to have wings but not able to fly. Just like them.” He said this with near reverence as he took his hand and stroked one of the ostriches on the back.

Before Grace could reply Star continued with a smile, “And so here, they wear a crown. Because they are the Queen of birds in my world.”

“Queen and not king?” she asked.

“Every king is a queen first.” He said it with a twinkle in his eyes.

Grace knew it was some kind of riddle and was trying to figure it out when he took her arm and whisked her away into another one of his rooms.

Star's room was as different as night and day from Kyle's. In fact, inside his room were other rooms. They had ceilings higher than Grace could possibly crank her neck to see and with the most ornate furnishings and colors. Plush and velvet fabrics. Exotic and intoxicating to take in.

And the music. The sensation of music here was on a level Grace had never quite experienced.

Star ushered her over to a plush, teal-colored couch and motioned for her to sit. He took a seat across from her in a chair that had a back as high as her eye could see. He looked tiny in it, yet somehow perfect too.

"Let's talk," he said as he crossed his legs, his feet not able to touch the ground. It was then that Grace noticed he wore heels higher than she could believe were physically possible for a foot to wear.

"Perk here... can go as high as I want to go," he said smiling.

Grace sighed, "I don't mean to sound ungrateful... but do you think maybe you could just tell me some things? Kyle made me ask the questions this morning, and with all I've seen and felt so far, my brain is mush. I can't even think of a thing to ask and yet, I want to ask everything."

With the most compassion Grace had ever felt from someone he said, "I totally get you. I'm proud you have lasted this long here. Why don't you lay down there, on the couch and get comfortable my love? I will tell you a story."

Grace welcomed the suggestion and stretched her body out along the soft and cushioned couch. Star tucked a pillow under her head as he patted it with his other hand. He plopped back up in his chair and waited for her to settle in.

He spoke slowly, "Now close your eyes and listen very deeply to what I'm about to tell you." Grace already felt hypnotized by just those few words.

Star continued to speak slowly, "Grace, you have been given permission to see something that a lot of living beings have yet to see. The truth of all humanity. Since the beginning of time, humans have been told a lie. And that lie, in part, was for their own good. Humanity was not ready to know the truth. And that was part of the process. And it wasn't that they were out-and-out lied to. It was, let's say, a lie of omission.

"You see, every human feels the lie the moment they take their first breath. And throughout childhood, they have glimpses of the truth. But the lie is so strong because it is what can be seen with the human eye. It can be touched. Experienced. And so... the truth begins to dwindle from each child. Some sooner than others. Until the lie is all that remains in each one. The journey is all about humans finding a way to, in each lifetime, shed the lie more and more."

Star paused to let Grace catch up with what he'd just said. Grace's eyelids felt like they carried the weight of the world, and she couldn't open them. He could feel her though, and when he felt she was ready, he continued.

"Grace, have you figured out what the lie is yet?"

Grace could barely bring herself to speak, but somehow her mouth moved on its own as she said, "That there is no life and there is no death?"

As soon as the words came out of her mouth Star sat up straight, as if he'd been electrically prodded. He put both of his hands to his mouth and clapped as gleefully as if he'd just discovered and unwrapped the present he'd been waiting for.

"Yes, baby girl! Yes!" Star exclaimed.

Groggily, Grace replied, "I still have no idea what that means though."

He whispered in her ear, suddenly right next to her, "Oh sugar, you don't have to know what that means. The fact that you even understand to that level is enough to change the world." And with that, he snapped his fingers and Grace, once again, crashed back into her body.

She stared at the ceiling, also feeling like she'd been prodded with electricity. She was wide awake, unlike other times where it takes a while for her to gather her bearings. This time was different. Way different. Just as she was about to sit up in her bed, she heard Star's voice and laughter echo from far away...

"Welcome to the 5th dimension baby!"

CHAPTER 8

Grace found herself in the hallway of the mansion. It was as if she'd just plopped down into it. She had no recollection of falling asleep prior... or any travel to it.

There she stood, alone. There was no sign of Kyle. No sign of Star. Just her and a hallway that went on forever. Grace observed with her peripheral vision how the hallway walls appeared to be plain white and empty on both sides. But as soon as she would turn her head left or right to look down the hall, doorways appeared on each side as far as she could see. It was a really trippy feeling.

She decided to go to the left, and as she began walking she could swear that the doors morphed into faces. She was initially shocked and didn't realize the magic in it...the fact that she actually recognized the faces.

Grace walked through the door and into a room that was incredible. It was bohemian in feel. There was a blue macaw parrot in a cage. There were peacock feathers in various places. Hanging tapestries. Red. Orange. Purple. Teal-green. Every hue of blue. Carpets and curtains and throw pillows. Chaise lounges and tables that were low to the ground. It looked as if a party should be going on there... yet, the room was empty minus the macaw and Grace.

She could hear footsteps, but she couldn't tell where they were coming from. She whirled around to the left and to the right... front and behind, and no one was in sight. Yet, the footsteps seemed to be coming from all around her. Right when Grace was starting to feel fear over her lack of control in not being able to see where they were coming from, she appeared right in front of Grace's face. A woman Grace instantly recognized, not so much by her face (she was standing so close it was hard to focus), but more from the woman's attire. Or maybe it was her energy. Or maybe it was everything.

Grace was stunned, unable to move or speak.

"You've seen how many spirits, and I am the one that gets your tongue, girl?" The woman laughed as she spoke, while simultaneously bringing Grace in for a huge hug. Even though Grace couldn't feel the woman's physical body, she could feel her energy and intent, including her vibration, which was as delightful as it was electric!

"Wow..." was all Grace could respond.

They stood staring at each other, smiling. Grace felt such love emanating to her, from this being... it was pure bliss.

"I just can't believe I'm standing here with you. I mean, I didn't expect this at all... you at all," Grace stuttered.

The woman joked, not at all poking at Grace, but elbowing her as she said it, "Yeah, that kind of scares me considering you're a Seer."

Grace laughed. "Wow... just wow. Janet Japlar. I have so many thoughts running through my mind right now..." Grace found herself getting lost in the various thoughts and questions swimming around in her head.

"Well, the beauty in that is we have all the time in the galaxy to get to them," Janet said, sitting down on a chaise lounge and gesturing for Grace to join her.

"I've waited a long time for this, you know," Janet said, drinking a mug of hot tea.

Noticing Grace staring in awe at the sudden appearance of a steaming cup of tea she said, "You want one of these?"

Before Grace could reply, Janet said, "Get ready baby, it's hot." And with that, she snapped her fingers, and Grace found herself holding a hot tea, too. And she was right, it was hot. It was the craziest thing to feel. A non-physical thing... and yet she could feel it as if it were actually there.

Grace shook her head as she felt overcome with emotion. "I just want to say thank you so much... for being here... for sitting here right now with me... for this tea..." Grace laughed at the last part as she raised her cup in a cheers motion.

"I have to say, it makes me happy that out of the boys around ya, it's me that gets you all moved and teary-eyed and such," Janet replied.

Grace almost snorted at what Janet said, as she said it right when Grace was feeling one of those waves of emotion and sipping tea at the same time. It shocked her that if she imagined sipping the tea, she felt it as if she actually was. It wasn't like there was actual tea there in a cup... or a cup for that matter.

"Or is there?" Janet asked, reading Grace's thoughts.

Before Grace could reply, Janet slapped her on the leg and said, "That's a whole other topic for a whole other time!"

Janet laughed at the look of relief on Grace's face, which made Grace start to laugh too.

Grace didn't feel like she could handle the enormity of that conversation right now.

"Let's talk about some things, shall we? To start... girl... I've been watching your love life over the years. What a ride!" Janet said.

Grace was stunned and speechless. First, that Janet said she had been watching her over the years... second, that she wanted to start on that topic!

"Wow... umm... well, yes... it's been a ride this lifetime, that's for sure," was all Grace could muster to say.

Janet leaned forward and put her hand on Grace's leg, and with all the compassion in the world said, "That's cause you keep pickin' the men that want to drive."

Grace stared into Janet's eyes. They were full of wisdom. Like staring into Merlin's eyes or, as silly as it sounded, the eyes of a bald eagle. There was just a palpable knowing in them that put Grace at ease and helped her to feel she wasn't at all being criticized.

"These men... they want you on their terms, and believe me sister, those terms are set in stone unless they evolve overnight. And we both know that ain't happening. At the same time, your relationships have been absolutely in line with your own evolution... and also, helping them with theirs. No mistakes. No regrets. But maybe next time, attract a man who doesn't need to drive or have you drive. Pick one that is beyond the confines of the vehicle of masculinity. One who doesn't identify with control, but rather the free flow of the heart. Where wholeness is the driver of the vehicle of your connection."

Janet added, with a grin, "Better yet, ditch the vehicle and be in the vast expanse of free love. That kind of magic ride is what you're ready for, baby."

Grace knew every word to be true, and before she could thank her for the wisdom, Janet interrupted with a "No need to thank me! Not anything you don't already know, girl. You just needed a reminder," she said with a wink.

Grace leaned back against the wall that the chaise was pushed up against. She could feel the cold concrete through her shirt and smiled at the thought of Janet Japlan having concrete walls in her 'heaven.'

"Keeps the cool in," Janet said, once again reading Grace's mind and winking.

"Makes sense to me!" Grace laughed, resigning to the fact that everything here was just going to have to make sense, or else nothing would.

The mood shifted, and Grace could feel it. There was a more serious tone in the air, and she could tell that Janet wanted to speak about something deep, or at least more than the small-talk and men-talk they'd been having so far.

"It's a time right now, sister. Whew... ever a time. There's a real battle right now, and it isn't in the sense of how you view battle. Earth's version of battle is a winner and a loser. Winning or defeat. This battle rises above the duality of either. It is most necessary. And you know that saying... that it's going to get worse before it gets better...?" She paused making sure Grace was keeping up.

There was a seriousness to Janet that made Grace feel a brief moment of dread as if she could foresee or feel just how much worse it could get.

"The only thing to dread, sweet girl, is what it feels like when you don't answer the call. You're answering. So are many others," she said as she looked deeply into Grace's eyes.

Grace understood what Janet was trying to tell her. She didn't exactly know how she did, but the understanding was deep.

"Now... I know there are some things you want to ask me..." Janet said in a mischievous tone.

"Uh sure..." Grace stumbled on her words as she was struggling to switch gears from topics.

Grace hesitated, not quite sure how to word her question correctly. "I guess my first question is if you are at all connected to a God or are one... what are you?"

"Well baby, I'm really connected to Neptune. And so is another spirit you are going to meet down the hall. I bet you'll know the moment you feel him," she answered with a sly smile.

"Wow... that's incredible... what exactly does that mean? I'm asking honestly... why Neptune? What does it mean?" Grace asked, feeling a little frustrated with herself at the limitations of her mind and ability to comprehend any of this at all.

"You could say we like to gather the fish," Janet said, laughing as she did. She was tickled with herself.

"'We' being you and the other spirit I will meet down the hall?" Grace asked.

"You got it! We had a following baby girl. Did we ever! And he more so than I... since I left body well before him," Janet answered.

"Can we talk about that? Why you left body as young as you did and how?" Grace asked cautiously.

"Sure baby! Nothing is off limits here. You know... we ain't any different than any other that comes to planet earth. Granted, we remember a bit more... but even that is unconscious remembering. The energy that surges through us is so intense, it has to be released somewhere, and so you have what makes us different than some of the rest when it comes to the prolific ways in which we channeled that energy. But other than that, we forget just like every other soul. That we are Divine. That we are there for a purpose. The mission. It is imprinted in our being... but that doesn't mean we don't get lost like everyone else. In fact, we may have gotten lost more. Even though we didn't remember with our minds, our souls did, and so, we were always chasin' that Divine high.

"And man did I chase it. Booze, drugs, sex... anything I could do to bring it back. And it was never enough. Always fleeting... so therein lies the vicious cycle. But man did I have fun. I really did. I loved every moment of it. And it was my time to leave. It wouldn't have happened if it wasn't. A lot of us, we left around the same age. Right before they could get a hold of us or use us for something other than the mission." Her answer was reflective and made Grace a bit sad.

"Don't cry for me Argentina!" Janet blurted out.

"You know that song? That was well past your time!" Grace smiled.

"Oh, we keep up on the music. We also help inspire some of the songs that you've heard since we left. We're always working from here baby... always. This one, in particular, is just a catchy tune. I like to sing it with wild abandon as I fly down the hallway. So many of the others don't really care for it. So, it's a real hoot to pull their chain!" Janet answered through genuine laughter.

Grace felt a surge of love in her heart. Just comfort and love and like she wanted to reach out and hug Janet.

Janet read her mind, "You can hug me, sister, get over here!"

As Grace wrapped her arms around a now very physical feeling Janet, she crashed into her body and bed in a flash.

All Grace could do was stare up at the ceiling. How would she ever explain to anyone what she was experiencing? How would anyone ever believe her or even be able to get it for a second of time?

As she tried to catch her breath from the incredibly detailed and fantastic time she had just spent, somewhere outside of this realm, she had one thought…

"Who the fuck needs drugs when you've got this??"

CHAPTER 9

Grace woke up in her bed to the feeling of someone being in her room. She didn't feel any fear. She recognized the energy immediately, and as her eyes came into focus, she saw him sitting in front of her bed.

She instantly smiled, and he smiled back to her, neither one of them speaking.

Grace lifted her upper body off the bed and braced herself on her forearms as she said, "I don't know what to ask you first... why are you here or where did you find the chair you are sitting on?"

"I will start with the easy part first, Grace, so you can grasp it because I know you don't do well with comprehending prior coffee intake. I thought the chair into reality," Kyle answered, legs crossed, still smiling.

Grace chuckled and asked, "So is it here or not here?"

This made Kyle smile as he answered, "Look at you... wanting to jump straight to the hard stuff. We can get into that after you actually have some understanding of what you're learning lately, Gracie."

Grace smiled at him calling her Gracie. His way of telling her 'not yet grasshopper'.

Conceding, she asked, "Okay then... why are you here and me not there?"

"What? Am I not welcome here anymore? Now I have to let you know I'm coming in advance? Or only see you in my realm?" Kyle teased.

"Very funny. You know you're always welcome here, even though your visits have been far and fewer between," Grace said in a jokingly jabbing way.

Kyle smiled, "You know, I find it cute that you miss me. I mean, you still have a life to lead, and here you are, missing little ol' me." He sarcastically put his hand over his chest as if he was humbled to the core.

"You know, I find it cute that you have a whole galaxy to play in and yet, you miss me enough to keep coming back here..." she bantered back.

"Touche' Grace... touche'...now, the reason I'm here. I thought I would escort you this time. You know, my version of coming to pick you up thing," he said as he looked her in the eyes.

Grace could instantly tell he was keeping something from her.

"Nice try mister. As flattering as that would be, you're not a very good liar. Try again," she said flatly, making sure he knew she meant it.

He continued to just look at her, and she could tell that he was contemplating whether or not to tell her, or whether she would ever take anything but the truth for an answer.

Before he could decide she said, “You know how stubborn I am. You might as well just tell me. I'm not going to be able to let it go!”

“Damn, you're annoying sometimes Grace,” he said, half-jokingly.

“True... not the first time I've heard that. But you know what? This thing we have here is based on trust, and how can I trust if you aren’t telling me everything?” she asked sincerely.

“Isn’t that the whole point of trust? Not knowing everything, but having the faith to trust that the person who isn't telling you everything is doing it for your own good thing?” he quipped back.

“I suppose... but I’m still not letting it go,” she said.

“Look, we all just decided that an escort right now would be a good thing. You aren’t exactly flying under the radar right now, Grace. It's more for your protection and less about anything other than taking precautions,” he said, hoping that was going to be enough for her.

“And they sent you??” she asked sarcastically.

“Haha asshole. I’m just the only one you can see,” he replied, and with that, Grace suddenly saw the room filled with angelic beings and ancestors and even some tiny elemental beings. The moment she saw them, they disappeared. Just like fireflies.

“Okay. That was pretty badass. I don’t know whether to fall to my knees in thanks or pass out from fear that this is necessary right now,” Grace whispered.

“Don’t be a drama queen,” Kyle jokingly said while rolling his eyes at her.

He always managed to make her laugh, even in the more frightening and overwhelming times.

“So, what do we do then? How are we doing this?” she asked.

“Well, you're going back to sleep. We're doing the rest,” Kyle answered.

“But I don’t feel like...” Before she could finish her sentence, Kyle had raised his hand and appeared to be blowing her a kiss. What he was really doing, was knocking her into another realm.

Grace didn’t remember any of the travel or the other beings. She had no idea how much time had passed or how long she'd been asleep before she found herself standing at that all familiar gate. Staring up at that all familiar staircase. She heard the wind blowing through the tall oaks around the mansion and the sound of distant wind chimes again.

She stood waiting to see if Kyle would appear. Or Mercury. Or anyone. But no one did. She decided to proceed through the gate and up the stairs, doing her usual landmine dance around the papers on the ground, careful not to step on or disturb any of them.

She got to the front door and wondered if she still needed to knock or if the door would be unlocked for her. She decided to try the latter and turned the gigantic doorknob. It was indeed open, and she peeked inside before walking through it. There was no one in the front entryway, so she decided to step in. As she did, the door closed by itself behind her. For some, that might have freaked them out. For her, it was a sign that they had been expecting her and that she didn't overstep by letting herself in.

She made her way to the red-carpeted hallway and began to walk down it. With each step she became more disconnected from her physical senses, moving into a dream state. So far no doors were appearing, which she found perplexing. She continued to walk and realized maybe her doing so was getting her to the state she needed to be in. Just as she had the thought, she saw a doorway appear up ahead, on the left side of the hallway.

It seemed like it took an eternity for her to get to it. Like she was walking in slow motion, or her steps were getting her nowhere. She eventually made it through. She turned and stood before it, waiting for a face to appear as it had with Janet Japlan's door. Nothing was happening, and just as Grace was about to knock, the little wooden window opened, and a living yellow canary slid forward like a cuckoo clock. It was the cutest thing she had ever seen. As she stood mesmerized and fixated on it, the door creaked open.

Grace was both stunned and amazed at who stood before her. She had started listening to his music later in her life, once she began recognizing the genuinely prolific musicians...the ones who were most definitely channeling through their bodies on stage. His vocal range was most impressive. So was his ability to mesmerize.

To her, he was pure magic, and she was in awe that he was standing in front of her at that moment.

Sheepishly, yet with a twinkle in his eye, he said, "Welcome dear, I'm Frankie Jupiter."

Grace laughed, a little out of nervousness and also at the absurdity that he felt he needed to tell her who he was.

Laughing nervously Grace said, "Thank you, I don't really know what to say right now."

This made Frankie smile as he said, "Well that makes two of us. Truthfully, I haven't had much experience visiting with humans. This is equally interesting for me," he said with a smile.

Grace noticed he was smoking a cigarette and he motioned for her to come into a front room that looked like a tavern. It felt like they were underground... in a basement bar...like a speakeasy. It was cozy and private and felt very French to her.

He sat on a bench, which was backed up against a wall that looked like it was made of stone. There was a round wooden table and a wooden chair for Grace to sit in. The chair had a latticed back and again reminded Grace of the French bistros she had visited while in France.

Grace sat down and asked, "So out of curiosity, why the French feel?"

"Just to piss off the British," he joked as he flicked the ashes from his cigarette into a black ashtray. "No seriously, because I know you like that feel. And most people would expect something closer to a Swiss feel. So, in other words, just to keep people guessing, including you." He winked as he said it.

"If you don't mind me asking, why have you not visited many humans since you left? I mean, knowing what I know now... that so many do and have. Why not you?" she asked.

"You know you are bringing back memories of what I hated the most about being Frankie Jupiter." He replied. Grace could not tell if he was being serious or joking by his tone.

"I'm sorry for that," Grace said sheepishly.

"It's okay dear... I'm mostly teasing. Although I did sincerely dislike the interview parts of that lifetime. Which leads me to answer your question. In all honesty, I wasn't fond of too many people when in my body. That wasn't a judgment as much as it was the deep inner world I liked to stay within. Private...you know? That may seem ridiculous to some considering my persona when performing. But it was so. I wasn't a very social person. But if I liked you... or even loved you... it was eternal. And I have a few of those I have visited since being out of body. Otherwise I quite like the realms I'm in right now."

He quickly added, "You aren't going to see me 'haunting' just for the sake of it!"

Grace noticed the smile on his face as he contemplated what he had just said. So she waited, feeling he was going to keep talking, and to her delight he did.

"Haunting. Such a strange way to put it. We are born into Earth. We leave our bodily shells there. We leave all our possessions. We are forever connected in fragments of our lifetimes. To say revisiting or staying close to someone or something there is 'haunting' ...it really is just visiting. I mean, if you go back home to see your childhood neighborhood are you haunting it? You're revisiting. Reflecting. Reconnecting. The dead and the living both do it. The only difference is the belief in the dead and the living."

"This is something that has been brought up to me since visiting here. And I think I understand it on basic levels, but it does go against the primal part of my being... the death and life thing and the illusion of both," Grace stated.

"It really is quite simple darling. Leave it to the earthlings to overthink it all. Say there is energy... a collection of energy that makes up a spirit... and as soon as that energy enters the 3rd dimension, it transmutes into matter. And when it leaves the 3rd dimension, it transmutes back into pure energy... because outside of 3rd dimension, that's all that exists. Would you say the matter is the most real one? Or the pure energy? Neither are...in the context of what humans want to call dead or alive," he answered, with genuine compassion and not in a condescending way, which he very well could have considering Grace was struggling to grasp the concept.

Frankie read Grace's thoughts and said, "Oh dear heart, we don't criticize or judge humans. We were once human. Many times. There is nothing to criticize. It's a beautiful state of being. Just as where we are now is a beautiful state of being. None better than the other."

He took a long drag from his cigarette as he said this. "And you...you darling will be where I am, and I will be where you are once again. It is forever changing, just like costumes. That's all that death and life is... wild costumes!" Frankie added.

Grace smiled at the thought of what he was explaining. She could feel the deeper parts of her soul remembering this.

They sat looking at each other, neither feeling the necessity to speak.

Grace decided to eventually break the ice by joking, "That is one eternal cigarette you have there."

Frankie laughed, "One of the perks about where we are. Anything can last as long as you wish, or as short as you wish."

"Do you mind me asking what God you're associated with?" Grace asked. "And what about Goddesses?"

"Oh, we are all connected with a Goddess and a God. Again, what has been translated into the human text are two separate deities. When in truth, it's the flip side of a coin. One in the same. I'm part of Apollo," he answered, and as he did, rays and beams of golden light poured out from him.

Grace felt goosebumps all over her body as the energy of warm, golden light swept over her skin. It was like being cold and suddenly feeling the warmest air envelope you instantly.

"That was beautiful, thank you!" Grace said, graciously.

He replied with a smile, "Who doesn't like a little sun?"

As Grace pondered the question, her thoughts were brought back to the time Mercury had visited and took her to see the giant switchboard with just a few remaining lights lit up.

"Ah yes... we come back to the subject at hand. Don't overthink that too much. Your mission isn't to change that. Your mission is to come to an awareness of truth so that others will follow suit. We're watching and handling the rest. We have a whole host of Divine beings doing the same. And Source...what you call God in all your different ways...is on point too. The world is on time. It may seem like things are spinning out of control, but it's on time. You must trust this.

"Even how music is being manipulated today. Humans are completely unaware they are being subliminally brainwashed. Manipulated. Hypnotized. Influenced. America being the command central of this. It will not be enough to throw the mission off track. Oh, they try to, and they give great effort, as we give great effort. But in the end, we are giving it together... and that is the resistance that brings humanity to the evolution needed for the next level. It's all beautiful. All of it." His eyes were ablaze like he had two suns in place of them.

His words sank deep. So deep...and as they did, Grace's eyelids began to feel like lead blankets. It wasn't until she heard him whisper, "Rest now darling. I will see you again soon, I'm more than sure of it," and with that, she realized she was back in her bed. Her head pressed against her soft pillow. Covers up and around her tightly, like she'd been tucked in. Grace couldn't fight it. She fell into a deep and restful sleep and was almost certain that she was smiling as she did.

CHAPTER 10

The room was stark white, just like the first room Grace had found herself in when Mercury first came to her. This room was giant and had floor-to-ceiling windows at the back of it. Grace could see what looked like a tropical jungle that was expansive. It felt like this room was in the center of the rainforest.

The walls had various tribal masks. Some were ornate and beautiful, and some were downright fierce which made Grace want to look away.

There was a beautiful couch. A leather sectional that was pure white. All Grace could think of was how if she had that couch, it would have been stained on the first day. This one, however, was stark and spotless.

Grace noticed that the white marble floors were covered almost entirely with various animal skins. It perplexed Grace, and as she was lost deep in thought, she heard a voice thunder from behind her "All of those died natural deaths and are Sacred."

Grace was hesitant to turn around. The voice dripped with an authoritative tone and caused little shivers to race up and down her spine. As she slowly turned around, she saw him standing there, smiling. He had a 'gotcha' look in his eyes. He was wearing a long-sleeved white linen shirt and matching linen pants. He was barefoot and glowed with a golden light that surrounded him from head to toe.

"You were scared. Admit it!" His words were laced with mischief, and he had a look of pride on his face. He was quite taken with his own thunderous voice, it seemed.

Grace couldn't help but laugh as she replied, "Yes... you definitely had me there."

They stood there briefly...just assessing each other before he walked down the few foyer stairs and passed by her on his way to the couch.

"On any given day you may see a jaguar... a tiger... all kinds of things out these windows," he said while sitting down and gesturing for her to join him.

Grace slowly made her way over to the couch, and in the time it took to get there, she'd already walked over a tiger, a leopard and maybe a bear skin.

She sat down next to him holding her hands in her lap, a bit nervous and reserved.

"You can call me T, if you were wondering," he said, breaking the awkward silence.

"I was, thank you. Thanks for having me here too... it is an honor," she said softly.

"And if you don't mind me asking right away... what God or Goddess are you connected to?" For whatever reason, it was the very first thing Grace was curious to know.

"Kali."

"Kali? The Goddess of destruction and change?" Grace asked.

This made T smile as he responded, "Kali, Kali, Kali. Change, change, change. Ain't ever met a hustler who ain't chasing strange."

"Strange meaning, new?" Grace suddenly felt stupid even asking the question.

"Yeah, somethin' like that. Change ushers in the new. New always proceeds change. Kali always demanding that change," T replied.

"That's what my life was all about. Bringing about the change. Calling out what needed to change. Standing up and sometimes that brought about the destruction. Even of my own life. But I was never afraid of destruction. I was afraid of being like them. The ones who refused to change. To evolve. The ones who thought they had the whole world fooled. Speaking out of both sides of their mouth. Saying they were for the people when really they were only for themselves." His intensity came out as he spoke.

Grace couldn't put her finger on whether he was angry or if it was just part of that life force that she knew was a part of the representation of Kali. She had studied some in her years and had witnessed the energy first hand in her own life. The archetype was strong, and anyone in its path was not going to get out unscathed.

"See... whatchu thinking right there... that's a misconception about Kali," he said pointing at her as he said it.

Grace looked at him without speaking, sincerely wanting to hear what he was going to say next.

"Destruction is beautiful. Chaos is beautiful. Every single part of it, beautiful. It isn't as if this stuff happens for no reason. Everyone thinks if it's dark, or what is considered bad... unfair... change... loss... the void... it must be terrible. It's just as beautiful as the light, good, fair, gain, expanse," he said passionately.

"That is really difficult for any human to grasp or even get on board with. I mean, we feel... we hurt... it is primal," she answered back.

"I get it... I was the same when I was in body. What I created was me working all that out. You know? I rapped about the struggle for the truth. I look back now and see that so much of me was just Kali in flow... but I was still human. Just like you right now. I still had that primal sense and belief in the duality. One over the other. One or the other. No other way." T looked away as he said this. As if he was deep in thought about that particular lifetime.

"I was getting too loud. I was about to explode. After all that went down. The energy was building up. Big time. Shoot, they thought I was vocal before. Oh boy... I had big plans." His smile had a tinge of sneakiness, and that made Grace smile. Here he was sitting before her in his Divine form, and she could still see glimpses of him being able to reconnect with the human existence.

"Did you have any idea that it was coming?" Grace asked.

"I could feel something on my heels, yeah. Like a heat... like a breath... like something stalking me. I was conscious of that, but that ego... it can really take over, and I was angry. I was angry that night too, and that clouded my senses. Looking back, you know, I can see how I felt it right there." He turned and looked out the giant windows like he was hoping for one of those tigers or jaguars to appear.

"In the other places I have been here, it seems like whatever is thought can appear instantly. Can't you just make them appear?" Grace asked.

"Yeah, but what's the fun in that?" T replied, not taking his eyes off the trees and brush. Looking for any sign of movement.

Some time passed in silence before he turned to her and smiled. Grace couldn't read the look she saw in his eyes. It seemed a mix of compassion and maybe a little sympathy too.

"I was at the front lines with the others. Each one played their role and got us to where the planet is right now. Some musicians are still playing their part now, for sure. Most of them are flying just under the radar. The ones who weren't, well... you know what happened to them. That's why it has now expanded to all those humans awakened enough to stand on the front lines with those who remain. You are one of those. There are many. You can't lose heart now. I feel you, and I can feel you are getting beaten down.

"You just remember Kali got your back. You call on Kali. She will handle them. She will handle all that tries to bring you down." His tone was serious, and his words were concise.

"Thank you for that. I will remember, I promise. But what is the end game here? That's where I get the most overwhelmed. Where is this all heading to? I mean, I can feel where we are going... I just don't understand how it's possible, or what needs to happen to get us there." Her voice trailed off, she was sincerely heavy in heart over the thoughts.

"I know I'm going to sound like a punk saying this, but it ain't for you to know, Grace. You can't look at the end game. You gotta keep your eyes on the present. One moment at a time. I know that's a lot harder said than done. Trust me. But you got this. You wouldn't be here otherwise." T stood up when he said this and walked a few feet from the couch.

Right when Grace was going to stand up, thinking maybe their time was up, she saw T shapeshift into a black panther. Grace's natural reaction was to leap from the couch and in one swoop, over the back of it, to have some kind of barrier between the two. The panther crouched, staring at her as a peal of laughter echoed throughout the room. The echo continued, and at first, Grace was pissed because she could literally feel her heart in her throat and her legs felt like noodles trying to hold her up. But as the laughter continued, she couldn't help but start laughing too, and while she was laughing so hard that she had to hold her stomach, T shapeshifted back into his original form.

He was still laughing, wiping pretend tears from his eyes, "Oh Grace... thank you for that. I haven't gotten to do that to a human yet. I do it to these clowns all the time with no reaction. I'm gonna remember that for a long time."

Grace stood up from behind the couch, adjusting what appeared to be her jostled clothing and hair and said, "Glad I could oblige."

She walked to the center of the room where he stood and looked deeply into his eyes. He had such resilience. Such a powerful, yet gentle energy. Out of all those she'd had the honor of meeting so far, he was leaving her with a real hope that she could get through this time of transition.

He smiled as he read her thoughts and as she began to feel sleepy, he said "Now, I know you got a personal friend there, back on the planet, who loves me. You tell her I got her back too, hear?" He said it as he put one hand on her back and the other over her third eye, like he was about to baptize her. And as he bent her back, she fell into her bed softly and deeply into sleep again.

CHAPTER 11

"I can feel you stewing," Kyle said through the darkness. "Talk to me."

"I don't even know where I would begin, seriously. I'm just done. Toast," Grace replied, not turning towards where she heard his voice coming from.

"You're not even going to look at me?" He asked, almost sheepishly.

Grace never could turn her back on him, literally and figuratively, so she rolled over to face him. As soon as she did, tears welled up in her eyes. She had been so drained, so beside herself it had gotten to the point where no tears were coming. Now, she felt them rushing forward like a raging river, and nothing was going to stop them.

He smiled lovingly, with the compassion of the higher being he had become. The ascended being he had returned to.

No one spoke. The only sound was Grace's runny nose and a few sobs in between.

"What has you most upset, Grace?" he asked with compassion and sincerity in wanting to know.

"It's everything. What happened to you. Still not seeing your truth out after how hard we are all working to stand up, and by it. Feeling it all. Dealing with the implications of what that has brought into my own life. Losing faith. People throwing hate my way. Not fully understanding what is being shown to me. Or understanding it somewhat, but the patterns are so set..." she mumbled, not finishing the rest of her sentence. She was too tired to continue.

"All of this is because you, Grace, are trying to solve it all, carry it all, do it all, and that is where you are wearing yourself down. No one expects this of you. Not me, not those in the mission, not Source, no one. You couldn't if you tried for the rest of your days, Grace. Change your view, and you will see how off it is right now. You know I appreciate it all, but I've been trying to show you a different way, and you keep reverting back to this. Don't you trust me?" he asked, staring straight into her eyes.

"Of course I do. You know I do. I just feel this boomerang feeling inside of me, where as soon as I begin to really get... like truly get... all of this, it returns back to wanting to be asleep. And angry. And in the duality. And the belief I can make a difference, or even should. I feel like a mess. A giant fucking mess and it's getting worse as I'm having these amazing experiences. And then I feel like a giant asshole because I'm having these experiences and should be so humbled and honored and happy. Instead, I feel so out of control and hopeless." Her words poured out with sincerity.

"One shift, one little shift Grace and it will all be in place for you. I promise you. Don't give up now. You are so close to truly seeing. Do you trust me right now? Will you go with me to talk with someone?" he asked her.

“Now?” she asked, sincerely hoping for some sleep.

“Now.”

“Okay, I want to see it from the view you are speaking of. I do. I'm ready for that... at least I feel I am.” Even this she was questioning.

“Close your eyes and concentrate on your breath. Even, in and out. I'm right here with you, and we are going to go together. Surrender and go to that place you know so well. Look at that. You've always been able to get to that place, your whole lifetime. There is a lot to trust in, even now in the middle of this so-called mess.” He sounded like he was reading from a bedtime story and it was making Grace drift more profoundly and deeper within.

Grace smiled and whispered, “This is the longest I have ever seen you not swear.”

“Concentrate, Grace. There will be plenty of time for fuckery later,” he smiled.

This made Grace laugh, and that was all she needed to fall back into the deepest sense of peace within. It was just there, right under the layers of all that she was resisting within.

She found herself with Kyle in the red-carpeted hallway, having skipped the entire front gate and steps leading up to the mansion.

They wandered down the hallway, Kyle walking just a notch ahead of her on her right side. When they got to a door on the left side of the hall, he motioned for her to go ahead of him. She turned around to look at Kyle, and he answered her question as it formed in her mind. He then gestured for her to open the door... that she didn't need to knock.

Grace turned the gold and ornate doorknob and found herself standing outside. This wasn't an indoor room. It looked like a nature reserve. There were beautiful trees and paths winding in and out of them. Grace could hear birds singing. She saw all kinds of wildlife. The sun was shining brightly through deep-set trees. The sky was blue with fluffy white clouds speckled throughout.

She felt such peace. Such love. Such light, and right when she was going to say something to Kyle, she turned around and noticed he had walked to the right, some ways ahead of her. She followed, and they entered a path into the woods. The route was winding and narrow. Kyle was ahead of her as she slowly walked while taking in her surroundings.

Finally, they arrived at a break in the path. It led into a circle that had rows and rows of beautiful rose bushes. It was here that Grace looked down and noticed both her and Kyle were suddenly barefoot. They stepped into the circle, and Grace touched the softest and warmest sand underneath her feet. It instantly warmed her from the outside in. They continued to the center of the vast circle, making their way through the paths between the rows of rose bushes. In the very center of the circle was a white blanket and white throw pillows. A man was sitting with his back to them. He was seated meditation style, Grace could tell. He had long brown hair, just past his shoulders. He was facing the back of the circle, where there was a huge fountain of water streaming out of the mouths of dolphins and mermaids.

Kyle went to the right side of the man and sat down, and as he did, he gestured for Grace to go to the left. Grace hesitantly sat at the left of the man, trying not to turn and stare at him so she could see who he was. He felt familiar to her, and she had an idea, but she didn't want to assume.

"Ahh, the old 'no making an ass of you or me,'" the man said in his English accent, without turning to her.

Grace immediately felt overwhelmed. He was exactly who she thought he was, and the energy emanating from him and Kyle, and even the forest, was vibrating so high it almost left her dizzy and feeling like she could pass out.

"Don't worry, you will acclimate in just a moment," he said, turning to look at her with the most loving smile.

"Hello," was all Grace could think to say back.

The man laughed and said, "Well hello there, Grace." He turned and looked at Kyle, and they both smiled at the silliness of the moment.

He had been a part of an absolute phenomenon in rock music. He was one of those musicians who came on the scene at the earliest stages of the mission. His band had taken over the world really. He was shot and killed, and though Grace was only six at the time, she remembered it.

Grace turned her body towards him as she just stared at both he and Kyle. Their energies were so similar. Maybe not as much in their respective physical lifetimes, but in this realm their energies were comparable.

"Kyle tells me you've been a bit tethered by the grips of confusion lately. Would you allow me to assist you with that?" he asked.

"I would be honored and grateful," she answered as tears began to flow down her cheeks. Embarrassed at her sudden flood of emotion, Grace quickly wiped them, and as she did, he grabbed her hand to stop her.

"First, tears are gifts. Don't be ashamed of them or hide them," the man said.

He spoke to her softly, "One way to help you view your confusion in a different light, is first to acknowledge that there is an error in your thinking. This releases you from the grip of the lower self that tries to hang onto the confusion as a safety net. Just in case you're wrong about what you're thinking or believing. So let's start there."

He was looking at her as if he was waiting for her to do just that, so she said, "I acknowledge there is an error in thinking that is leading to my confusion."

"Good. Now, that error in thinking is the way you are viewing good and bad. Light and dark. Love and hate. Truth and lie. Life and death. Right now you are viewing it as two separate entities. Two opposing forces, correct?" he asked.

"Yes, most certainly. It's hard for me to view it any other way... much less the rest of humanity. I think it is the consensus." Grace looked down and at the pristine white blanket, contemplating the law of duality.

"This is true, every human under the laws of 3rd dimension has viewed it as such since the beginning of time. Every religion has taught it as well to some point. The concept of sin. Light and dark. You know what always makes me laugh is how we send Masters down to your Earth and most of them, in an effort to love unconditionally, hide away in a monastic life or on a mountain somewhere," he snorted as he continued, "I always say, yeah mate it's easy for you to love unconditionally locked away in a room or away from the everyday behavior of humankind. Try being human and see how fast that fails," he elbowed Kyle as he said this.

Grace had never considered this, but it was true to some extent. Jesus was a Master who sat and spent time with those that were judged and persecuted by the religious sect. To her, he was one who chose to engage outside of those realms.

"Yes, he did. And still, so much is hidden about his life on Earth," he said, reading her mind again.

"So the question here is, how do you begin to live within the paradox? Instead of outside the paradox and in turn, a constant victim of its torture? Well, it's quite simple, you see. Humans want to complicate it so much, and it really is the most simple visual.

"Let's take the visual of a recording studio. The majority of people may have seen a recording studio at one time in their lives, and if not, they can look it up and find an image of one. And for those who have no means to look it up, let's just assume they collectively receive the clarity as the mass consciousness receives it, shall we. Yes, okay... imagine the soundboard with me. All those knobs slide up and down. Each one is controlling a specific instrument or vocal on the track they are recording. Let's imagine that duality is one of those knobs on a single panel. The slide goes from zero to ten. And depending on what you want to hear, you choose where to slide that knob on the panel. Duality is one linear wave. Do you understand this so far? It's one line that goes from zero to ten. Zero, let's say is dark. Ten is light. And the rest is every shade in between. Some like to stay in the lower range. Some in the higher. Some right in between. The human chooses this, either through the karma... or the subconscious or conscious. But it's all the same. It is not separate. It is not two different or distinct things. It is ONE. And it all serves a purpose, depending on what is being played. Sometimes it has to be zero, or one or three. Sometimes it is to be eight or nine or ten. Sometimes it is right in the middle. But it is one. Do you understand this so far, Grace?" he asked, somewhat passionately.

"Yes, yes I do," Grace answered with excitement. She genuinely understood it, so far.

"Okay then, let's imagine a giant soundboard. And every human is one of those individual rows on a giant board. Each human is set at its own level in the scheme of duality, and all are playing a giant symphony on the planet. That is the big picture, go back to the individual row and remember that duality is not two sides. It is one line, and there are various levels to it. This doesn't mean you have to accept dark and stay there. Or hate. Or lies. It only means, that until it is understood in the paradox, there is always an illusion of separation created and therefore, judgment.

"And that means you stay stuck in the illusion, and life gives you another chance to realize it. Over and over again. Once you realize it is all one, without judging any point in that from zero to ten, only then can you choose where you want to set the knob. And when you come across another human that is set at a zero or such... in that lower realm... you can just simply say 'hmmm... that is interesting they are set at that part of the panel... they must be serving a purpose of some kind,' and go about your business without buying into theirs or trying to change their dial. Eventually, those living in the lower level will be able to see yours set higher and may decide they want to see what that is all about for themselves. And eventually, there won't even be a panel anymore, as the 3rd passes into higher dimensions where this 'duality' transmutes to ALL that is," he said.

"But again, let me add, the end goal shouldn't be to raise everyone to a ten, but rather, understand that zero to ten is all the same line. Not separate. Not two different things. The same exact line from beginning to end," he smiled at this last bit of information.

Both he and Kyle stared at Grace as she processed all that was just explained to her.

"Well?" Kyle asked her.

"Umm... mind blown," she replied.

"Oh good, yes, mind blown is the best place to be! Get that thing out of the way, and you will catch up quickly to all you are receiving," he turned his head to Kyle and smiled before looking forward and resuming his meditation pose.

"Next time you are presented with a human living zero through three, let's say for example… remember this visual. All one line. All one," he said, before closing his eyes.

Grace wanted to ask him which God or Goddess he was associated with, but in her heart, she felt it wasn't necessary. Somehow, he felt connected with them all.

And with that, Grace was out of the forest, away from both him and Kyle and back in her bed.

She sat up in her bed and really began to let it all sink in so she wouldn't forget it come the next day.

She could hear Kyle, but she couldn't see him as he said, "Sorry for the abrupt goodbye. He and I don't get a lot of time together, so had to boot you out," he laughed as he said it.

As she was about to answer Kyle, she heard him say "Goodnight Gracie," and he was out of the realm of her being able to feel or hear him.

Just as well, she thought. There was no way she could handle more conversation. Right now, all she wanted to do was let it sink in and set her free for good.

CHAPTER 12

Grace could hear the sound of the ocean as she started to come out of her deep sleep. It took her a few moments to focus her eyes on her surroundings. The walls were pale yellow, and she recognized the small cot she was sleeping in immediately. She raised her head up just enough to see Kyle in his regular place on the floor, with his back up against the wall and playing his guitar. The melody was a beautiful one, almost hypnotic, and Grace decided to move into a position where she could lay comfortably under the warm blanket and watch him play.

"Do you know what one of my favorite things about being here is?" He softly asked without looking at her.

"It's gotta be this cozy twin cot," Grace answered, laughing.

This made Kyle look at her and smile a look of sarcastic approval as he answered, "Every note... I can hear in ways that are far beyond what I could when I was in my body. The way a melody falls, if I had breath, it would be taken," he answered playing more passionately and loudly as he did.

Grace tried to focus on each note and experience what he was, but somehow she knew she wasn't quite getting it.

"It's as if each note is suspended for a moment... and pours out to the next... and all of that I can individualize and hear without compromising the timing. Pretty cool shit," Kyle said.

"Could you imagine if we could do that on Earth? Music is already the most powerful and moving force. It would be so hard not to listen to it 24/7 in that case," she said.

"People would shut the fuck up, and that would help the planet a lot." His dry response made Grace smile.

"Truth," she said.

"So... what's on the agenda? I've learned enough to know I'm not here just to hang out with you," she said, looking at him in anticipation.

He shot her an exaggerated look of pain as if she had hurt his feelings.

She knew he was teasing her but she added, "You know I love hanging out with you..."

His smile was one of satisfaction as if he had gotten her to admit to something, "You're about to meet with someone extraordinary, Grace."

"As if I already haven't been doing just that?" She was overwhelmed at even the thought of what or who was next.

"Yeah, but this one doesn't hang out here. He has his own planet, and he came here just for this. We've all been catching up with him. It's not often we get to," he said while fidgeting with the tuners on his guitar.

Before Grace could gather her thoughts or ask her next question, Kyle was gone. He just disappeared, leaving Grace alone in the room. Something in her knew she needed to get up and wait for this being, whoever he was.

Grace had an idea, but she had learned not to think she had any of this figured out... it almost felt disrespectful to assume anything.

She had her back to the door and was looking out the expansive windows at the ocean when she heard someone enter the room. She turned around and saw him standing there gleaming. He was like a star, pulsating beams of light. His smile too was just as blinding.

He gestured for her to make her way to the small table and two chairs that had suddenly appeared in the room.

Grace did it without saying anything. She wouldn't have been able to speak even if she wanted to.

Grace looked into his eyes for the first time, and he still had the signature one blue eye and one brown eye.

Grace couldn't help but laugh a nervous laugh as she cupped her hands to her face in disbelief.

"I just can't even comprehend that I'm here right now... I can't..." she said shaking her head in disbelief.

“That’s quite okay, take your time,” he said, studying her closely like he was scanning every speck of her being and energy.

If it had been any other person, she would have been uncomfortable, as it almost felt like he could eat her… sizing her up for a delightful human snack.

This made him laugh, he was reading her thoughts. He was amused at her musings and was still smiling when he said, “Oh Grace, nothing to be scared of. I don’t eat humans.”

His smile was radiant and full as he said this. Not the least bit offended by Grace's observation.

“If it helps you out at all, we too are quite overwhelmed to be able to communicate with those beyond the realms. Especially if that communication is clearer than we are accustomed to,” he said sweetly.

“I don’t see how that could be possible, but it does help me feel a little less… what is the word…” Grace was trying to grasp the word as he finished her sentence for her, ‘Inundated?’”

“Maybe… yes…I suppose. But I'm so grateful to be overwhelmed and have this to even deal with!” she said with complete sincerity.

“Yes, it's a bit like fame was, really. You have this part that is otherworldly and surreal, and yet, you also have the ‘deal with’ part too,” his tone was understanding and gentle. Grace felt he was so kind to come down to a simple level. She could sense he was. She could feel his absolute brilliance, and here he was, coming to her point of understanding and being perfectly happy to do so.

"Did you enjoy your lifetime? The one I know you from?" she asked.

"Oh yes, most certainly. I enjoyed every moment of it. Even the not so enjoyable ones. I really was able to complete my mission and also, enjoy my time as a human being," his answer was nostalgic and genuine.

"What was your mission, if you don't mind me asking you?" Grace said.

"To expand the newly laid foundation of the mission in music. To expand the way it's done. To expand the way people viewed labels... male... female. To open people's minds and in a lot of ways, pour the energy of the cosmos into them," he answered.

"I can really see that clearly now... now that I have become aware of the mission. You were brilliant," Grace looked at him as she spoke and saw the sweetest look in his eyes.

"Thank you, Grace. I think you're quite brilliant too. All human beings are. Every last one," he said.

Grace laughed under her breath as she could think of a few she didn't find so brilliant and then felt guilty the moment she did.

"Oh, you are perfectly allowed to feel that way! In fact, it's healthy to allow yourself to. Otherwise, you suppress all that needs to come out, hindering your progress in getting to the place of true freedom on Earth. There is nothing wrong with thinking they aren't brilliant because at that moment you are considering how they are really choosing not to be. The key though is in the understanding that even when they're choosing not to be, they are still a brilliant embodiment of Divinity and nothing could ever change that. No matter how dark a person chooses to be... how far in the underbelly they have traveled. Nothing can ever separate them from what and who and where they come from," his tone was serious but still kind.

It made complete sense to Grace, and she was beginning to feel the healing taking place in her own body and mind. As she was learning from all of them, she was learning to love herself and see herself through their eyes... the way they viewed human beings. It was amazing and humbling to feel.

"You know what I like about you Grace... you flit like I did. You have really done well in your life trying new things... new places... new forms of expression. You've reinvented yourself time and time again, just like I and so many others did when they were in body. It shows your connection to the Source and knowing it is always seeking new ways of expressing yourself. That stagnant energy does not behoove the person who is unwilling to change or reinvent. You should be quite grateful that you had that inner knowing... as it's half the battle won," he said with a smile.

Grace thought about that for a moment. Sometimes she had been critical of her changing with the winds... feeling the call to new and different and wanting to express and create in those aspects. One thing was true, and that is Grace never abandoned any of the ways in which she chose to create. She would always return to them again. Her life was rich with experiences. Rich with love. Rich with connection, and she was beginning to fully understand that, and in doing so, started feeling intense waves of gratitude well up and move through her.

“And that, too, is something we love... how deeply you can feel. Did you know there aren't a lot of humans that can feel as much?” he asked her, staring straight into her eyes.

“Maybe not consciously, but I did have a hard time the first 20 or so years of life with realizing that not everyone feels as deeply or at all. It took a long time for me to understand that... and then I went through a time where I questioned if I was defective because I could,” her voice had a tinge of sadness as she recalled some of her struggles throughout her lifetime, on the way to self-accepting.

“Don’t be sad at those times. They were great teachers and each person that didn’t return your feelings or couldn’t understand your ability to feel so deeply, was simply mirroring to you how special it is to be able to. The gift in it. And it's taken you most of your life to get to the point where that mirror is helping you see this, instead of automatically turning on yourself and feeling like there is something innately wrong in you, because someone else isn’t your exact match in thinking and feeling,” he sat in silence for a moment before he continued.

“Now the world is full of more empathetic tones and shades, and now you can really see the contrast of those who feel and those who don’t. But each time you allow yourself to be you, you're helping someone else get in touch with that part of their being. Even if it is unconsciously... so don’t stop. For the love of the sun and stars... don’t stop,” he said with conviction.

This brought tears to Grace’s eyes and she felt a lump in her throat when she tried to swallow and speak.

"By the way, did you know I come to Earth often?" he said, fully knowing she was unable to speak at the moment and changing the topic at hand to a lighter one.

Grace wiped away the few tears that had trickled down her face as she said, "You do?? That's amazing!"

"Oh yes... anytime you see a meteorite in the news, that may be me!" His grin was mischievous and sparkled brightly.

Grace giggled at that and asked, "What do you come back for?"

"To help those still on their missions. I have a favorite I come to often... she's a powerhouse, and I like to send her blasts of inspiration and energy. I'm not sure she knows it's me though," he laughed as he said this.

"Do I know who she is?" Grace asked, sincerely curious.

"Yes, you used to sing her songs as a little girl. She and her sister..." he said waiting for it to hit Grace who he was speaking of.

Grace's eyes got as big as saucers as she said, "Really?? I always knew she was powerful!"

"Yes, quite... she is a force," he said with a smile as he continued, "There are more I come back to assist. I also assist the planet in any way I can when I'm in the zone," he said as he motioned his hand like it was riding a wave.

Grace was trying hard to take it all in and not lose focus on the importance of what she was being allowed to know and experience... it was just all so much. Even thinking of him coming into the atmosphere and how this was all connected and tied together. It was a lot to take in.

"One thing to remember, Grace, is that even though we all had our missions, and we all stayed connected to Source, we still lived life. We lived it to the fullest. There's a difference between morality and integrity and all too often, humans want to bind the two as one... like you can't have one without the other. Morality is based on duality. Integrity is based on being true to oneself. There's a difference," he said.

"Live by being true to yourself," he said as he began to stand up. "And I will come to see you on my next trip around the sun," he said with a beautiful smile and tenderness in his voice.

And with that, Grace found herself alone again and extremely sleepy. She waited to see if Kyle was returning, but her eyes were getting heavier with each passing second. She decided to go lie back down on the comfy cot, and as soon as she did, she was falling as fast as the meteorite he'd spoken of.

As Grace drifted off to sleep she could hear what sounded like sparkling stars falling... she didn't know how that could be... but it sounded like star showers, and it was heavenly.

CHAPTER 13

Grace found herself sitting in a chair that was fit for a queen. She had no recollection of how she got there, and as she focused on the details of her surroundings, she had to catch her breath in amazement.

The chair she sat in was made of what looked like pure gold. It had a high back and reminded Grace of royalty. Looking around she saw more elaborate pieces made of the same gold. Elegant peacocks were strutting around the room, and the theme was reminiscent of ancient Egypt. To Grace's surprise, there were also black cats lounging throughout, but they were bigger than typical house cats, and they also got along peacefully with the peacocks. It gave Grace chills to feel deep within her soul something so familiar about the whole room. It was as if she remembered parts and where things were positioned before she ever laid eyes on them. This was beyond déjà vu. This was the most intense remembering she had ever experienced, yet she couldn't quite put her finger on how she remembered it. Like there was a veil between her and the memories.

Without warning, she appeared. Grace initially thought she was seeing Cleopatra with her jet black hair. Her style was reminiscent of the images depicted of Cleopatra throughout history. She was wearing a sheer sleeveless dress down to her ankles. Her waist was adorned with a gold rope that tightened over her skinny torso. The dress had high slits up both sides that allowed the fabric to float slightly behind her in a most haunting way. As she got closer, it registered with Grace who she was.

"Oh my goodness... I just watched a documentary about you! I thought you were Cleopatra just now!" Grace couldn't help but hide her glee. She had an incredible amount of respect for this old soul and her short time on the planet.

"There is a reason you saw her first, love," she winked.

"Wait, so you're saying you..." Grace looked confused as she was trying to grasp what was being implied.

"Yeah, doll, one in the same," she smiled and plopped down on a plush velvet chase. At the same time, she snapped her fingers, and an ancient pharaoh-looking man appeared to light her cigarette.

"It's the shit, right? Get ya anything you think of," she said like a child in a candy store.

Grace was amazed. It took her a few moments to gather herself enough to concentrate.

"So, what do I call you? By your name or Cleopatra or..." Grace didn't complete her sentence hoping there would be more divulging on past lives.

"Oh, I don't give two fucks straight about what you call me now. Makeup something!" the woman said.

"Might be stupid, but how about Jazzy? Since I know that energy oozed from you in your most recent lifetime," Grace softly spoke, feeling a bit embarrassed at the suggestion.

"No... no don't be embarrassed. I can dig it. Jazzy. Yeah, let's call me Jazzy, just because you came up with it!" she said. She flicked her ashes into the air, and they just disappeared as quickly as they appeared.

"Okay then... Jazzy... wow... I'm honored and grateful to be here. I feel you have so much wisdom that didn't get to come out fully in your lifetime and it's such an honor..." Grace stumbled over her words.

"Oh doll, likewise. You know, I look back and see what was supposed to come out, did. I didn't fully realize my mission until after I left. But man, was I happy to go. I was like shouting 'fuck yeah' as I entered this realm. Entirely and utterly ready to piss out of there," she said.

Grace found it interesting that she was speaking through the persona of her last lifetime and not Cleopatra, but right when she was thinking this Jazzy interrupted her thoughts and said, "Cleopatra was much saltier babe. Much."

This made Grace laugh... somehow, she could envision that.

"No one got why I was there. Not one person. For some, I existed to sing. For others, I was a best friend or a crush. And then there were those who saw me as their opportunity. But not one person got why I was there," she said shaking her head.

"And why were you there? I have a vague idea of what your mission was, after watching you perform and hearing you interviewed. I picked up a lot, but I'm not sure I'm in the right vein there," Grace answered humbly.

"You are, you get it. I feel your imprint of thoughts and feelings. On point. I was there to mirror to humans their incessant need to put someone up on a pedestal and lose their minds over someone they view as famous. Even when that person is druggin' out and drunk as shit, and even when that person is obviously dying in front of their very eyes. The public knows that all a musician wants is time alone to create, yet they pay no mind because there's an addiction and high achieved when we worship those we feel are better versions of who we could ever be. And for most people, better only means rich or famous." Jazzy looked down as she said this. Grace felt a ping in her heart... she could feel how much Jazzy suffered in that lifetime.

"You know, I was meant to kind of mirror to the people and let them wake up from that a bit. I only knew how to be me. And I was a direct channel to that which is raw and real. Messy. That was the mirror. It was like my whole life was saying to other humans to fucking get real. Be raw. Be the channel you can be. Stop losing yourself to another human and instead focus on yourself and what you came here to be. I was also mirroring that in my love life. I lost myself. I was so in love with love. I felt it to my bones. The whole thing feels like it got lost in translation. The purpose of it. You know?" She looked up at Grace when she asked this, and again Grace felt a ping in her heart.

"Well, maybe the message of your life is something that is going to become clear to others down the road as the world awakens more? I certainly hope so," Grace answered.

"Yeah doll, you never know. It's something that's out of our hands once we leave. None of it matters once we leave our body. I came into the world, in that lifetime, and did what I was supposed to... and left when I was supposed to. It is what it is and always was and will be," Jazzy said.

"The world just wasn't ready for you yet," Grace joked.

"The world's on time, love," she answered back.

"You know, they offered me the opportunity to come back... into body... right away..." she quickly said.

"And you said no, no, no?" Grace said with a smile.

"Clever girl!" Jazzy said, looking genuinely proud of Grace for her attempt at humor.

"So if you were Cleopatra in a past life... what God or Goddess are you connected to?" Grace asked, very curious to hear.

"I'm connected to Mut, Mother Goddess," she answered quickly.

Grace smiled as she heard this, having remembered reading quite a bit about Mut on her travels to Egypt.

Jazzy interrupted Grace's nostalgia. "You haven't picked up on something yet. A surprise for you."

Grace thought for a moment... and then said, "Does it have anything to do with why I find this room familiar?"

"Quick as a whip! Yes, do you remember?" Jazzy asked.

"Not exactly... I mean, I do deep inside but maybe not consciously," Grace muttered.

As soon as Grace said that, Jazzy smiled a sneaky smile and sauntered over to the front door. Grace watched as Jazzy opened the front door to Kyle standing on the other side.

As soon as Grace saw Kyle a heartfelt wave of remembering welled up from a place within her being that she'd never felt before. It felt like the most Sacred tunnel of her being, never previously accessed in this lifetime, and just now coming to light. The wave was so intense, it flowed from Grace in the form of tears.

Grace watched her tears flood the floor and trickle towards the front door where Jazzy and Kyle stood. Grace felt like she'd just ventured down a rabbit hole of experience, and she was Alice in Wonderland. She saw crocodiles swim in the water that was formed from her tears. The room transformed into the banks of the Nile. Grace, no longer on a chaise lounge, was now on a wooden raft that floated in the water.

Jazzy disappeared into thin air before Grace's eyes, and only Kyle remained, just outside the doorway, which now appeared to be the other side of the riverbank. He stared intently at Grace as image after image passed through her third eye of their lifetime in Egypt together. Who he was. Who she was. What they looked like. All emotions felt... all memories realized.

Just as Grace felt she was going to be taken over by a feeling so intense that she felt fear in surrendering to it, a gush of water pushed the raft forward, and Grace felt her body crash back into her own bed.

She sat up in bed gasping for breath, feeling quite panicked, until she heard his voice. He wasn't visibly around, but she could hear him say, "Sorry Grace, I know that was a shit ton. You were ready though. You needed to see that."

"And feel it? I feel like I was just slapped silly by the hand of God or something. As beautiful as it was to experience, it was terrifying on 10,000 levels!" Grace said. It was truly abrupt and mind-melting.

"Oh come on, didn't you like being back?" Kyle asked.

"Yes, yes... I just wish I'd had more time to get used to it so I could really experience it without feeling fearful," she answered.

"If that were allowed you wouldn't want to come back to your life as Grace. Trust me on that. Just sit with what you did see and allow it to speak to you. You're going to need to remember who you are and who you were soon," his voice was grave and at first, which made Grace nervous. Until she realized all of this was beyond any of her control and now, more than ever, trust was required for the journey.

"Exactly... trust and remember. You will dream more about it as time goes on. You remembered, and now there is no stopping it. Now go the fuck to sleep," Kyle said, making Grace laugh out loud which in turn conjured up feelings of peace and love... enough to fall asleep.

CHAPTER 14

Grace was back in Kyle's room. This time she was sitting on the floor with him. It only took her a split second to realize where she was, prompting her to comment, "I wish these landings were a bit more smooth..."

"Where's the fun in that? I love watching your clumsy entrance. It's one of my favorite things. You do it void of any finesse or grace..." he said sarcastically.

"Nice." Grace acknowledged Kyle's play on words.

Grace noticed a cat in the room, which made her light up instantly.

"You have a guest today..." she said, petting the feline as it purred.

"He's no guest. He's been with me in almost every lifetime," Kyle said smiling.

"Why am I just now seeing him?" Grace asked.

"Because you needed it today," Kyle said sweetly.

"Well thank you for that... it's true. I do," Grace said.

“He has magic medicine in him. Just let him do his thing... and you will feel much better,” Kyle said, watching as the cat chose to jump up on the cot and stare at the both of them, as cats often do.

Grace could swear she saw the cat grin at her... and before she could say anything Kyle said, “Told ya.”

Grace beamed and looked at Kyle for a bit before asking, “So why am I here?”

“Again with the ‘why-am-I-here’ question. Can’t you ever just let something unfold naturally?” Kyle said. Grace could detect that he wasn’t joking.

“I can... but it's hard for me, as you know,” Grace admitted, knowing all too well her endless questions were one of his pet peeves.

“You're like a child on a road trip... are we there yet? Are we there yet?” he said, using a tone of voice that mimicked a small kid.

He looked up at Grace and smiled as she flipped him the bird. She knew he was right. She had been that way since she could remember. Christmas. Birthdays. Any surprise or thing she had anticipation for.

He just looked at her with both compassion and humor and smiled a patient smile which made Grace feel like he tolerated her... but was amused at the same time.

Without warning, Grace felt the air change and his energy turn more serious. She waited for him to speak and it seemed like an eternity before he did.

“Something that you don’t realize right now, Grace, is that they really can engineer anyone they want to,” he said in a tone that raised concern in Grace.

“What do you mean?” she whispered.

“Meaning there is a technology that's been created which can cause people to do things they normally wouldn’t do. And without going too deeply into that... music, mainstream music is being used in that way right now,” he said.

“How in the world is that even possible?” she asked, wide-eyed.

Electric waves... beams... is the easiest way to put it,” he said, indicating that ‘how’ they do it is irrelevant.

“What’s the purpose of it? I mean, I can let my imagination run wild with the myriad of things that could occur when technology is in the wrong hands,” she said solemnly.

“It's already in the wrong hands. There are actual people who you've seen do things to themselves, and others that were engineered to do so. This is why the mission has been accelerated. Do you understand?” He stared into her eyes, and in a way, Grace felt he was making sure she was getting it in the deepest sense of the words.

“I'm understanding, as mind-altering and frightening it is to hear,” she answered.

She sat staring down at the floor, lost in thought before she continued, “So many thoughts are flooding my brain right now. From this being used for mass control if people were to revolt, or there to be an uprising.”

“Yep, kind of gives a new meaning to the definition of zombie,” he flatly replied.

“So knowing this, what can be done right now? It kind of feels hopeless even thinking about it,” she said.

“It isn’t hopeless unless all the lights go out. And unless people don’t stop losing themselves to the fame train and worshiping those on it and start looking within themselves. Look, there was a time the fame thing was a way for The Opening to reach mass consciousness. Now, it has shifted, and The Opposing is using it to influence in the same way. Get it?” Kyle seemed a bit agitated when he said this, but Grace knew that was some of his Shamanic energy coming forward. He was a peaceful warrior at heart.

“So is the solution to counter The Opposing with those who are rising up now... those who are left... the lights on the switchboard I saw when Mercury first came to me?” she asked.

“That will help, yes. But the main solution, Grace, is just for people to wake the fuck up. We don’t have ‘time’ for anything other than that,” he said, actually using air quotes for the word ‘time.’

Grace laughed.

“What?” he asked.

“I don’t know... it's just funny seeing you use air quotes,” she said.

“Why?” he asked.

“I don’t know... you don’t seem like an air quote kind of guy to me, that’s all,” she responded with a smile of satisfaction. She could tell her teasing was getting somewhere.

“Well, that’s where you're wrong Grace. First of all, I'm not a ‘guy’ anymore,” he again used air quotes for the word ‘guy’ and in a very exaggerated way.

This made Grace laugh even harder as she replied, “This really gets to you... I can’t believe something as silly as air quotes has you right now.”

Realizing she wasn’t going to stop teasing him, he stood up and started to walk to the cot to pet the cat, turning his back entirely to her as he did.

She could still hear him though, which was his intention.

“Do you hear that fucker over there trying to make fun of me?” he said as he continued to pet the cat and ignore Grace.

Grace smiled even more.

She decided to get up and walk over to Kyle and throw her arms around the back of him as she simply said, “Thank you.”

"For what?" he asked, without turning around.

Grace let him go and said, "For always making me laugh. Even when we are talking end of the world kind of shit."

"This isn't end of the world shit Grace, this is a brand new beginning," he said as he turned to face her.

They looked at each other, neither one needing to speak for the moment until he broke the silence and said, "Thank you too."

"Okay... I'm going to bite even though it's against my better judgment. Thank you for what?" Grace hesitantly asked, sensing a set-up.

"For being such a fucker," and with that he pushed her forehead back with his hand, and Grace found herself booted out of his room and again in her own bed.

She giggled as she came to... he was such an ass at times, and she loved and appreciated it.

She heard his voice boom through the room as he said, "Likewise Gracie. Likewise."

CHAPTER 15

He was sitting in front of her when Grace opened her eyes. She once again found herself back at the mansion, not remembering how she got there. The room reminded her of Kyle's a bit. It was pretty minimal. It was small, and natural sunbeams were coming from small windows adorned with very delicate lace curtains that were long enough to puddle on the floor. There were live house plants throughout. Some were hanging from the wood-beamed ceiling. Some were set in planters of all colors and shapes. Grace noticed she was sitting on a brown couch. It was incredibly comfortable, and Grace could imagine herself napping on it. He was sitting in a rattan chair. She recognized him immediately.

As Grace looked around the room, she noticed there were four doors, which perplexed her. He read her thoughts and said, "My attempt at humor..." his voice was monotone, and he didn't smile when he said it.

Grace thought for a moment and laughed as she said, "I get it... your band."

He smiled and leaned forward to grab a pack of cigarettes from the glass coffee table in front of them.

Grace was watching him when he looked up and said, "It isn't that we actually need to smoke you know. It's a reminiscing."

"I get it," she quickly replied... not knowing what else to say in response.

"So you've been kept abreast of things, I'm hearing," he said looking up at Grace while slowly blowing smoke out of his nostrils. Grace noticed that his movements and speech were slow. No hurry or rush or even assertion.

"As much as I can handle, I guess," she replied.

"You know, I tried to talk about it when I was there. The beginnings of brainwashing via the radio. How they play the same songs and when you think of the many songs they could play from the many talented musicians, they play the same small amount. Over and over. Even then it had started. And it makes sense. When I was alive, the young people were catching on. There were protests and a desire or longing to break free from what that generation had intuitively felt as confinement," again, he spoke slowly. Grace was appreciative of this. It was such a broad subject for her to take in fully.

"You were very much a part of their awakening," she said.

"Well, me and the others. Yes. I saw what was going on. It was actually quite depressing for me at the end. Hence why drugs and alcohol were more prevalent at the end," he said.

"There are a lot of rumors about how you died. There was no autopsy or even a look into the events that surrounded your end," Grace said, more in the form of a question.

"The bottom line is that my time was complete. No need to dredge that up as it only fuels the distraction. My mission was complete. As were many of the others at a young age. Look at how many you've connected with already that were my age or just a few years younger when they departed," he said. His speech was again monotone. Grace liked how he really held no pretenses. You got what you got with him, and Grace felt that he was a sincere and wise soul.

"Are you worried about the fate of the world and where it's going?" she asked him.

"I would if I couldn't see the big picture. So much has to happen to get it to where it needs to be, and that is really ever-changing. Parallel outcomes all in one given moment of linear time, which only becomes a reality when the energy and focus are supported by mass consciousness. There is a lot up in the air, so to speak. But the end will be as we all know it to be," he flicked his ashes into an ashtray as he said this, looking down at them like as if deep in thought.

There was more authority in his voice now, "If people would just look inward, the spell cast... for lack of better wording... would dispel. Turn off the TV. Turn off mainstream music. Put the technology down. I spoke about this too... that there would be no turning back and there really isn't. The planet can't go back to where we were before the technology, but they can certainly choose to reconnect with their Divinity, and that is only going to happen by going within. That will create the awakening, and it will lift the veil from humanity's eyes. So many are blinded right now. If they could just see that what they idolized in me, and all the other musicians for that matter, is what they possess within themselves. We were in the flow. We were free to be one with that and unique in the expression of it. Each person has that ability. It is the birthright of every soul that comes into existence."

"Do you miss being alive?" Grace asked.

"I am alive," he responded, frankly.

This made Grace blush as she realized that what he was saying was true.

"I'm sorry... still on autopilot with the dead and alive thing," she said.

"No need to apologize. Soon it'll be as natural as that autopilot," he smiled lightly for the first time.

"There are a lot of plants to take care of here," Grace changed the subject.

"Well, here we can choose whatever we want to create. It's up to me whether I enjoy the act of taking care of plants or whether I want them to self-sustain," he answered.

Grace pondered that for a moment, trying to read which one she felt he chose. He looked at her inquisitively and asked, "Go ahead... which do you think I chose?"

"I feel you choose both. Sometimes, you take care of your plants. Sometimes they self-sustain," Grace said with a nervous smile. She hated to be wrong. After all, she was still human.

“Well aren’t you a mentalist,” he said with a grin.

“I like you, Grace. You have a calming way about you. It's almost like you belong here,” he said, looking deep into her eyes. Grace had learned when they look into your eyes that way, they are assisting her with understanding them on a soul level, as opposed to just the conscious level.

She didn’t quite understand what he meant by his last sentence and didn’t really want to follow it. Not yet, anyway.

He interrupted her thoughts and said, “Since I know you're going to ask... Horus. I'm associated with Horus.”

Grace beamed and said like a school girl in awe, “Totally... I can totally see that.” Horus had also been a part of Grace’s studies and fascinations when she traveled to Egypt.

He smiled back at her and was now studying her. It didn’t make Grace uncomfortable, but it did make her curious as to what he was gathering.

Before he could amuse her with an answer, one of the doors opened, and Grace looked up to see who was about to walk through it.

In walked a man that Grace knew by looks, but not so much by his music. They had named an ice cream after him, and his band had a massive cult following.

He felt jolly to Grace as he came over and plopped down on the couch next to her. He was an older man with a white beard and white hair. He wore glasses and had the most fantastic smile.

"I thought we could kill two birds with one stone here," he said smiling.

Both of their names had started with the same letter, and as Grace was about to ask them what she was to call them, they both said out loud "Horus and Neptune!"

Grace jumped in her skin when they said it; it was so authoritative and in sync.

"Okay... well obviously I know who Horus is since we were just discussing that. So you are obviously Neptune..." she said turning to the man who had just walked in and sat beside her.

"Sharp one," he said sarcastically.

Grace smiled and teased, "Hey, give me a break. This is a lot for a girl to take in."

"I know... I know," Neptune responded with a grin.

"Now I understand what Janet had tried to tell me about who I was going to meet later.. .the two of you being connected in the Neptune way." Grace said.

"Yep, we're both cut from the same cloth," he said.

Grace felt the desire to wrap her arms around Neptune and give him a huge hug. He just had that kind of energy that made her feel like he was a giant jolly soul.

"You can hug me!" he joked, reading her mind.

Grace felt like she was five and instantly scooted over to give him a big side hug. She wrapped her arms around his neck and placed her head on his shoulder.

He patted her arm, and she could feel him chuckling as he said to Horus, "How come you don't get this kind of response?"

Horus just stared at them both, Grace could tell he wanted to smile but was holding it back.

"We try to get this guy to lighten up all the time," Neptune said gesturing to Horus.

Grace thought it was amazing to watch them banter back and forth.

"Well, I really don't have anything to add here other than encourage you and let you know you're doing a great job so far, and we're all rooting for you!" Neptune said to Grace.

"Rooting for me?" Grace asked nervously.

"Don't sweat it kid... just stay on track and all will unfold as if by magic," Neptune said smiling.

"See ya!" he threw his hand back in a wave without looking back at Grace or Horus and was out the door before Grace could ask him anymore.

Grace turned and looked at Horus and knew she probably looked like a helpless animal surrounded on all sides because Horus, for the first time, softened his entire gaze and sat next to her. He put his arm around her shoulder, and the two of them just stared at the doors.

It seemed like there was a long moment of silence before he broke it to say, "Grace, I know it is difficult. It would be for me too if I were in your shoes. I mean, I was in your shoes, but I wasn't as conscious of it. You are going through this awake. That's the most brilliant part of the whole thing. You'll understand it all very soon. Don't rush it. Just trust us. As we trust you," he said patiently.

"Do I have a choice?" Grace asked, half-jokingly.

"You know the answer to that," he smiled and looked down at her and into her eyes. As soon as he did, Grace felt incredibly sleepy and closed her eyes... and with that, she was no longer in the room from their realm but back in her own.

CHAPTER 16

Grace awoke to the sound of ocean waves rolling onto the shore. When she inhaled deeply, she could smell the sea. The ground beneath her felt lumpy, and Grace realized she'd been asleep on a thin beach towel on top of the most brilliant white sand she had ever seen. She propped herself up onto her forearms to discover the sea was a beautiful turquoise blue... never had she seen such shades of blue. Above her head was a giant straw looking umbrella, its ends frayed and flapping in the breeze.

Grace looked to the left and right as far as her eye could see; no one was there. Not one single soul on the beach with her. As panic swept through her, she detected the faint sound of steel drums, which calmed her enough so she could catch her breath. Although this was different than any other room she'd visited in the mansion, considering it was a beach, she knew it was connected. Therefore, she knew she was safe.

Some time passed... how long, Grace had no clue. Time just didn't exist in this realm, and it was difficult to grasp, like sand slipping through one's hand. On that note, Grace decided to do just that and grabbed a handful of sand as she squeezed it tight and watched it funnel through her grip. She was staring at her hand when she detected the movement of something way down the beach coming towards her.

He was walking along the shoreline, taking his time. Bending over and picking up a shell here and there. Staring off into the ocean for a few moments before continuing his slow stroll toward Grace. He wore linen pants that were rolled up to his knees. He had on a long linen shirt that was unbuttoned down to his navel. Even from that distance, Grace observed shells around his neck, tied with rope. His long dreads moved lightly with the breeze.

Finally, he reached the blanket Grace sat upon and motioned if he could sit down and share it.

"Of course!" Grace said, moving back as far as she could to give him a comfortable space to sit.

They both sat Indian style, facing each other. He had a beautiful and joyous smile. Neither of them speaking... just smiling at each other.

Grace was the first to break the silence, "I have to say, this may be my favorite 'room' so far."

"Ah, yes... ocean girl... Cancer girl... mermaid Goddess" he put emphasis on the 'ddess' part as he spoke.

"I don't know if I would call myself mermaid Goddess... I have become scared of being in the ocean," she replied honestly.

"You're scared of what you cannot see. What you cannot control. If you would let go, you will swim in peace. In joy," he stared into her eyes, and she understood he was not just talking about in the ocean but in life.

"I understand... I do," she said. "But sometimes understanding just isn't enough," she laughed at her own fear, amused at the story.

"De human plight," he said nodding his head now to the steel drums still playing off in the distance.

Changing the subject, Grace decided to dive right into things, no pun intended.

"You were so very wise and prolific in your lifetime," she humbly expressed to him.

He spoke with authority, "No more than the others. Clear vision. I was speaking to the masses back then and addressing the issues that people on Earth are currently fixated on. The system. The disease. The group of characters in power who are making choices for the people, but it ain't for the people. Only benefiting themselves. Their pockets. Their power-hungry need and their thirst for greed. Those characters are there so that the opposite end of the spectrum, the masses, can choose to oppose what they represent. Their greed sheds light on all the alternatives. Options visible from the inside. People become unconscious, concentrating on things that are external from themselves. Fame did not get me. Fame gets the people worshiping the fame more than the ones who become famous. Most times. Stay within and you don't lose consciousness. Stay within you will have clear vision too. Stay within and you don't get caught up in the chains. You don't become a slave to the establishment. To government. To religion".

He continued, "The time is here, on your planet. The time has come where breaking free means ascension. Staying chained means most certain suffering. You say, well staying chained would imply suffering for anyone. But the difference is that the choice is in the hands of the chained. Now more than ever. The ability to see there is no such thing as a captor or being held captive. Only choice."

Now, more than ever, Grace got this. She finally was in the place that she understood this in a way that it was no longer just wishful thinking that one day she might arrive at this way of understanding. She was there, and she felt gratitude welling up within her heart and that automatically translated to tears welling up in her eyes.

"Ah sweet girl, you feel it. You get it. Let the feeling free. That's it. That's the connection. You're going to ask me who I'm connected to... I am connected to the ONE. The ONE that all others are created from. Source of all that is, that WHO," he responded.

"Do you think the world is going to get it in time?" Grace asked, worried it might not be so.

"De world is on time," he repeated just like some of the others had.

They continued in silence. Him looking at her, her looking at him. Grace felt he was transferring information to her. She could feel strange sensations and a buzzing in her head that felt electric.

He stood up to leave, and Grace began to stand up with him before he gestured for her to stay.

"Stay... let your downloads take place," he said with a big smile. Grace wanted to hug him, but took his advice and stayed seated on the blanket. She still felt electric pulsations and welcomed being close to the ground.

“See you soon, Grace,” was all he said as he disappeared before her eyes.

“Well, what did that mean?” She worriedly pondered. ‘See you soon’ as in I'm going to kick the bucket soon? Or ‘see you soon’ as in I'll be back for a visit?

Grace began to wonder why she even worried, either way. It was such a natural and primal thing. The fear of death. The belief in death. Each one of them had said over and over, and in their own way, that they are alive. They are alive, and in a way that insinuates a new paradigm shift in thinking because it challenges what humans currently believe death to be.

Grace knew in her heart that what she had been taught to believe about death was not true. She had always known this to some extent, being a person that believed and experienced the ability to communicate with those who were "dead" since childhood. Death only exists in the mind of the human being who still believes that the act of dying creates separation. Separation is the illusion 3rd dimension casts over all humans. This illusion keeps people from believing they can communicate or feel their loved ones that are no longer in body. The illusion that people who can communicate with the afterlife are either crazy, delusional, fraudulent or all three combined. The illusion that keeps people searching on the outside of themselves what they innately have on the inside. That connection that they seek that is right there flowing through them at all times. Akin to being blind, humans place all kinds of feelers on the outside to find their way, to see where to go. Those feelers always lead to outside sources that mimic Divinity. However, those outside sources always dissipate the moment they are experienced. If they would connect within, the torment in the dissipation of the connection they seek would cease. Because within, underneath all those external experiences, is the real connection that is constant and can always be tapped into. Yes, Grace knew there was nothing to fear... ever again. But convincing the most primal parts of her being this was indeed truth was a whole other beast.

When she felt calm enough to do so, she laid back down on the towel and let the sound of the waves and steel drums send her into the most peaceful sleep.

CHAPTER 17

There was a buzz in the air... not only in sound, but in feeling. Grace tried to trace where it was coming from. She was in her bedroom and about to go to sleep. It sounded like the buzz of a guitar amp, and Grace had that familiar feeling someone from another dimension was close by.

Grace closed her eyes and tried to feel it. It wasn't Kyle. It wasn't a spirit she had felt before. It was difficult to explain, but they all had their own unique feeling to them. No two the same. She didn't recognize it, but could feel it was a higher energy. Not one she needed to be on guard for or be worried about, and so she allowed herself to leave her waking self and travel into sleep state, knowing they were most likely waiting for that anyway.

Then she saw him. He was sitting on a chair in the corner of Grace's bedroom, and it looked like he was playing a game of solitaire. His hair was an exaggerated version of the fully grown out hairdo he wore at the beginning of his musical career. He had on purple pants and a brown top. He was a guitar god in his lifetime, and he was a magic man. At least that was how Grace always referred to him.

"I like that... Magic Man," he said, reading her mind and as he lifted a card from the table.

Grace sat up and smiled. She liked the comfort of her bed this time as opposed to the mansion.

"Yeah, I thought I would come check out your digs. We can check out mine later," he replied, still not looking up from his card game.

"You can join me if you want to," he said.

Grace got up and walked over to the empty chair across from him and sat down.

He smirked as he said, "So tell me, what have you noticed as the theme in all of our embodiments."

Grace thought for a moment and then said, "There are a couple of things I notice. First, you all channel. Watching all of you perform live, I pick up the same energy and same way you all connect and in a way, disappear into it. Second, you all said the same things in different ways. All about being true to yourself. Being free. Being oneself genuinely. Free thinkers. Free from establishment. Being one with each other and the planet. A lot of you died young. A lot of you did drugs," Grace laughed at the last part while he just stared at her.

"Heck, if I felt as connected as you all were, and had to deal with the 'sleeping' masses of this planet, I would have done drugs too," she joked.

This made him laugh, "It was funny at times. I didn't get as frustrated as others. I just laughed and got higher. The lower they got, the higher I got. Drugs or no drugs," he said. "But that was then. Now, drugs aren't needed. Today, anyone who wants to connect can. The planet has quickened. That makes it lighter. Higher. Easier. That's why they are trying to distract and control, now more than ever. Because it's that easy... and The Opposing... they don't want to lose the power. Once people realize they can connect themselves, once that is a mass decision, The Opposing ceases to exist. Light and dark become one and everyone is awake. No, they don't want that... they're fighting like all holy hell to stop it," he said, still smiling. It was like he was always smiling... even when he wasn't... you could still feel it.

"Those recent deaths on your planet of front liners in this mission? They're using those to divide people. And look at how it's working. Everyone fightin' and attacking people that are fighting for the same cause. Anything to keep the distraction. A feeding frenzy of everyone turning on each other. It's like soldiers turning on their brothers as if they are the enemy. Things have gotten that out of control. It's working so far, but not for long. I tell you what, it pissed that Kyle off. We will call him Kyle for ease of understanding... we call him something else. Anyway, to see people tearing each other apart. People only caring about winning. In the beginning it took a lot for him to stay higher. You know, when he was still earthbound and such. But now he stays out of it completely. He works from the highest plane possible and stays focused on the ascension. One day, people are going to understand this was a huge part of it. That's why we are all grateful for getting that message out to the world right now. Time to wake up!" he said. The Magic Man's arms were folded in his lap as he leaned back and relaxed.

"I question whether the majority of people on Earth right now are capable of grasping this... but I have to trust it's going to happen or you wouldn't be working so hard at the end here. And coming to people like me too," Grace said softly.

He smiled and said, "I was all about the freedom. I wanted color and joy and each person to feel the freedom to be what they were inside. To express from it. To trust it. Themselves. It was happening then. It's happening now. It will happen in the timing it's supposed to. Trust that," his voice softened.

"I look back to when I played the anthem, and to me it was a beautiful expression. To others of that time it was disrespectful. All I was doing was playing my guitar and being free. Anthems will fall. Systems will fall. Structures will fall. The opposite of all of them is freedom. Look at how long society and people have carried along, bound by the system. Since the beginning of time. Someone oppressed. It's time for freedom and slavery to ascend too. No more master. No more oppressor. No more victim. No more prisoner. Just love," his voice perked up with the mention of love and it made Grace feel happy.

"Now, you are about to have a visitor. I will let you be," he said.

"No checking out your digs?" Grace asked.

"You can stop by anytime you like. You'll find your way," he said smiling as his hand grabbed hers on the table. He gave it a loving squeeze and was gone faster than Grace could blink her eyes. Grace also realized she was back in her bed and not at the table. Something she had no memory of at all. The Magic Man had left so abruptly, Grace didn't get to ask him which God or Goddess he was connected to, but she had begun to realize they are all one in the same.

She waited and waited for who was coming, and the more she waited, the heavier her eyes became. Finally, she couldn't fight it any longer and she drifted off to sleep.

At some point in the night Grace stood in the hallway of the mansion. Feeling that familiar out-of-body sense. She saw Cole coming down the hallway toward her. It made her happy to see him and then, in the same moment, guilty! She had almost forgotten about him with the craziness she had been experiencing.

"Not to worry Grace. No hurt feelings," he said, as he reached out and hugged her.

It was so good to see him. He had always felt like a big brother to her. Strange, considering she was way older than he appeared to her and way older than when he left his body as Cole.

They started walking down the hall and Cole had both of his hands in his back pockets as they strolled leisurely.

They got to a door that had a giant rainbow painted across it. Grace instantly smiled and he smiled back saying, "Had to have a rainbow greeting you."

It reminded Grace of the image he had painted for her one of the last times he had come to her, a memory she found comforting.

They walked into a room that reminded Grace of something Leonardo da Vinci may have occupied back in the day.

"I will stop you right there, Grace. I know you're going to ask me who I'm connected to... just think of him... he's a big one," Cole said, reading her mind.

Grace knew they both had to have been connected to something higher, but she let it go at that and was in awe at even the thought of da Vinci and Cole being connected, but it made complete sense.

The room had old wooden floors and two windows framed in wood. The ceiling had beams, and there were easels located throughout where Cole had been painting on canvas. A mattress lay flush against the floor. The only thing that Grace observed to be more extravagant was his choice of blankets, which were strewn over different chairs and the bed.

"You know I like to be warm and comfortable," Cole joked.

"Tea?" he asked as he brought her over to a round kitchen table and pulled out a wooden chair for her to sit in. He was a gentleman, even though he wasn't even in his body anymore.

Within no time there was a teacup in front of Grace and Cole was pouring tea from an old kettle. He sat down in the chair next to her and poured himself a cup too.

"Well, you've been on a mindfuck as of late, haven't you?" He asked, half-joking and half-serious.

"To say the least!" Grace answered, taking a sip of the perfectly brewed tea.

"How are you coping with it all?" he asked like a psychologist would. She half expected him to pull out a spiral notepad and pen to jot down her answer.

This made her laugh as she thought about his question. No one had stopped to ask her that question, not even Grace herself.

"Umm, I'm not sure I am. I'm just going with a flow that feels very fate-like to me and not questioning it as I do, I guess," she honestly replied.

"Smart. Fighting it would cause suffering," he looked up and at her as he said this. Grace knew he was trying to tell her to continue going with it, no matter how difficult it got.

"Kyle probably wants to be the one to tell you this, but I'm going to anyway. We are all ascending together soon. All of us. To a higher realm than where we're currently residing. It's the only way to fully assist what is about to happen on the planet," his tone was serious.

Grace didn't take her eyes from him. She was trying to read if he was happy about it. If it was a good thing that they were all going to ascend.

Reading her thoughts, he answered, "I'm finally ready and yes, it's a good thing. The earth is going to feel it in a powerful way. It will be palpable. And it will be throughout the next couple of months."

Grace laughed a helpless laugh and responded, "Sometimes I wonder why in the world I would choose to be on Earth at this point in time. This shit is frightening. It really is."

Cole laughed, too, as he put his teacup down and said, "Shoot, right now is the best time to be on Earth. This is powerful, as scary as it is. And I'm not saying if I were there in body again that I would not be losing my shit right now. I probably would. Look at how sensitive I was when I was there. I get it. You must hang in there though. You chose this. You chose to be there right now. Trust your own being."

Just then, there was a knock on the door which slowly opened to Kyle standing in the doorway.

"Hey man, it's time," Kyle said to Cole, not looking at Grace. This made Grace nervous and right when she was going to speak up, Cole got up and put his hand on Grace's shoulder. He gave it a squeeze as he said, "It was good hanging for a bit." He lit a cigarette as he walked off and gave Kyle a hug in passing.

Kyle walked up, almost apprehensively, and sat in the chair next to Grace.

"Okay, what's going on... you're scaring me," Grace could read him like a book.

"I promise you, it's not what you're thinking. Nothing bad," he answered.

"Then why are you acting weird? Is it because Cole told me about you ascending?" she quickly asked.

"What? That fucker, I was going to tell you about that. No... it isn't that," he said.

"Then what is it?" she gently asked, trying hard not to push him into answering something he didn't want to.

"It's just your time here at the mansion is coming to a close, and I'm worried for you... that you are going to be sad and have that to deal with on top of everything else," he softly said, looking at her with true compassion.

"You know I worry about you, Grace. I should have more faith in you, considering. And I do. I just know how you feel things and this year has been more than most could handle," this time he looked away as he said this and Grace wondered if he was feeling guilty or something.

"No, I'm not. I just know all this started with me leaving and sometimes I wish it could have been another way. That it could be another way," he said, reading her. Without taking a moment he continued, "But that is just when I get back into the Kyle's way of thinking. It happens for a while after you leave a big lifetime. Especially when you stay close enough to it. I know things are as they were meant to be, and are meant to be," his tone turned powerful and less Kyle in that moment.

Grace didn't know what to say. She had felt before that it was goodbye for her and Kyle. Not in the eternal sense, but in the way they'd been able to communicate since he first came to her. This time though, she felt it was deeper.

"It isn't goodbye in the way you view it goofball. It's a different way of us being. That's all," he said, lightening the mood that had created a giant lump in Grace's throat.

“Come on, we have one last surprise for you before you go,” he said, taking her hand and yanking her up from her chair.

She could barely keep up with him as he raced down the hallway towards the front of the mansion. She could hear voices and music and laughter coming from outside the mansion entrance, in the front where she always entered.

She was about to ask him what was happening when they stopped at a swinging door, the kind you would see going into a kitchen.

Kyle let go of Grace’s hand and said, “Go in, someone is waiting for you.”

Grace looked at Kyle and could see he was excited for his surprise... or their surprise... whomever was behind it. He had a smile like it was Christmas morning and she knew that whatever or whoever was behind the door was going to make her happy.

She took a deep breath in and pushed open the door...

CHAPTER 18

Grace pushed open the door and walked in to see a man with his back to her. He was wearing a white chef's jacket and was humming and whistling as he chopped something that Grace only assumed was vegetables.

It couldn't be, Grace thought. First, why would he be here in a mansion full of musicians. second, he was fucking humming and whistling. Like a lighthearted elf.

"Because he was just as much a rock star as any of us," Kyle whispered. Grace didn't realize he had been standing behind her.

The man heard Kyle speak and turned around to face them. For the first time, Grace burst into complete tears. She put her hands over her face and just stared at him in utter shock, which made him laugh. He had his hands on his hips and smiled wide as he said, "Oh come on, knock it off. It's just me Grace." He opened his arms, gesturing for her to come and give him a hug.

He might as well have been Jesus in that moment. Grace felt a huge burst of energy bolt through her heart chakra as she made her way over to him and gave him the biggest hug she could conjure up.

"Speaking of Jesus, that's who I'm connected to. And to think of all the times I took his name in vain," he joked as he hugged her back.

Grace didn't know how to respond, so he continued, "Not the freak that religion claims Jesus to be. He is a whole other being. Jesus is as free as the come. Pure love baby," he said, still smiling.

"I don't know what to say to you right now." Grace was still eyeing him as if he was going to disappear or shapeshift into someone else and the joke was going to be on her. "I mean, you're smiling. You're happy. You're talking about Jesus," she said laughing through her words.

"I know, it's crazy, right? Happy as a clam," he replied sarcastically, grabbing a clamshell from the counter and holding it up as his example.

Grace wanted to ask him about his leaving, but he interrupted her before she could, "Now is not the time, Grace. There's so much to that. Take a look around you... there are so many you could still talk with. That have stories of their own."

Grace looked behind her and there stood beings she recognized but had not spoken with. One was a songwriter and DJ who just recently left the planet. He smiled at her when their eyes met and she telepathically heard him say, "They are covering their tracks, but the truth is here," and he pointed to his heart as he said this. Grace got tears in her eyes feeling the magic in his being and the intent in his energy. Grace's gaze moved to the back of the room where she recognized the man once known as "the king of rock n' roll" smiling at her. She had communicated with him before, maybe this was why he had not come to her in the mansion. There were so many of them, and as Grace turned to the man she was so shocked to see, the chef and author and truth sayer, she realized they were now in the front yard of the mansion.

She was dizzy with the energy that had transported all of them in one blink of an eye and it took a while for her to find her bearings. When she finally composed herself, she stood there, with her back close to the gate she always entered, staring at all of them in the front yard adjacent to the staircase leading to the mansion. There was a massive firepit in the center of the yard and the fire was dancing high into the air. They were all standing around talking with each other. Grace could feel so much love. Just pure love and happiness.

They were having a fucking BBQ. The thought made Grace laugh out loud.

She was lost in the feeling when she felt someone standing next to her and looked over to see Mercury there. His arms crossed in front of his chest, a look of pride on his face as he stared at all of them and then back at her.

"They wanted you to be here for this. To see them do this. Each one of us thanks you for your service and your continued devotion to the mission," Mercury's voice almost cracked as he said this. It made Grace want to fall to her knees in reverence, but instead, he turned her shoulders back to the mansion and she watched as each being walked up the stairwell to their specific headlined newspaper. One by one, they picked up their respective newspaper, walked to the fire and with great abandon, tossed it into the flames. Each time one of them threw their newspaper in, they all shouted a tribal chant that Grace could not understand in language, but she could feel it in her core.

They all had their unique and individual way of doing it. Some walked slowly, hands in pockets. Some danced. Some acted like they were picking up doggy doo-doo and holding their noses playfully, like the whole thing stank up a storm! It made Grace laugh and cry all at once.

Finally, Mercury took Grace by the elbow and gently led her to the stairs. There was one newspaper left, and when Grace looked down, it was a headline of all the names she had been called, and lies that had been fabricated since she took up the cause. Things that had hurt her more than they should have. Things that no longer hurt her because she had freed herself during her time here at the mansion, realizing that no compliment nor criticism was hers to carry.

Grace picked up her paper and walked over to the fire. All of them stood staring at her like proud parents watching their child on the verge of accomplishing an amazing feat. Grace took the time to look each one in the eyes, saying thank you with her heart and not her words. She looked over at Mercury last, and he nodded for her to go on... and so she threw her paper into the fire and when she did, she crashed back into her body.

She sat up in her bed, and what started off as sobbing turned into laughter... laughter so joyous... so happy that Grace felt her heart might explode from gratitude. There were no words she could ever say to thank them for the honor of all they had allowed her to experience. She knew this was just the beginning. She stood up in her bedroom and walked to her window, pulling back the lace curtains so she could see the moon and stars. It was an exceptionally bright night, and she could see clearly the constellations. The stars individually twinkled and Grace imagined it was each one of them waving hello, connecting with her in that brief moment.

Grace understood the work had just begun. That this wasn't the time to be lazy, to fall back into what she was before she went to the mansion for the first time... as if that would even be possible.

No, now was the time to stand. Not fight. All she had to do was stand in the truth of what she had been shown. Stand and live from that truth. The rest would take care of itself.

A resolve came over her, more powerful than ever before. It felt as though every one of her lifetimes had merged together. She was united within. She put her hand over her heart as she closed her eyes and whispered,

"This is the beginning, and this is the end. THIS is the ascension."

Made in the USA
San Bernardino, CA
11 September 2018